The Final Days of Kobold Kody's Frontier Exposition and Tonic Show

The Final Days of Kobold Kody's Frontier Exposition and Tonic Show

ELI HOROWITZ

PINK
NARCISSUS
PRESS

The Final Days of Kobold Kody's Frontier Exposition and Tonic Show
© 2023 Eli Horowitz

Cover design by Julie T. Horowitz

Published by Pink Narcissus Press
Massachusetts, USA
pinknarc.com

ISBN: 978-1-939056-20-7
First trade paperback edition: November 2023

"If the answer is infinite light, why do we sleep in the dark?"
—Paul Simon

THE FORTUNETELLER

I: THE VISION

Two days out from the capital, Andra has a vision. It is a bloody prophecy, as her visions often are. Yet this one is more. It is the beginning of the end for Kobold Kody's Frontier Exposition and Tonic Show.

There, in her vision, is the hand-painted sign at the Show's gate. There is a pair of goblins: a ticket-taker and a barker. Behind them, she sees the night progress in its ordinary way. Hucksters sell snakeoil potions and candies to the carnival-goers. Against their cries, music lurches giddy and trembling through the air. The freaks in the sideshow look daringly into the eyes of the milling crowds, who themselves appear warped and misshapen in the torchlit half-dark. Carnival-goers shriek and laugh wildly, and are delighted at their own wildness. Around them, the night is open and endless and patient. Its vast presence tames the Show at its edges.

Around the main stage, at the center of the Show, there is another quality altogether. The audience there has already seen the barbarian, the pyromancer, and Andra, the fortune-teller. Now, with their faces lit by true awe and peril, the motley spectators stand rapt. Inside the wide circle of their bodies, a panting carny with a mutilated hand tests his will against a beast the likes of which none would have credited as real without the evidence of their eyes. This is the act they have all come to see: the dragon-tamer.

But here Andra senses the heart of her vision—the unhappy end that always comes. She waits for the silvery creature to impale the dragon-tamer, or crush him underfoot, or for an errant burst of flame to burn him dry. Instead, the dragon-tamer reaches for his hip, pulls a flask to his lips, and drinks. Andra's chest aches. Twice more, the dragon-tamer drinks. Then he brings his hand to his mouth and coughs once. Andra sees blood on his palm. She sees the dragon-tamer fall to the ground, and she hears the audience gasp, most in shock but a few in cruel delight.

The last of her vision is a retreating blur of all that will follow. A barbarian bleeds on the sand. The goblins sing a funeral hymn. Elven eyes watch from the trees. An orc leaves to visit the dwarves and never comes back. A pyromancer walks into the welcoming sea. One by one, the threads of Kody's Show will come undone. Like a costume worn too long, they will come to tatters and drift away on whatever wind finds them first.

As her vision ends, the snap of burning wood close by calls her back to the present. She and several others are gathered around the Show's evening campfire. Jorg, the dragon-tamer, sits across from her, hunched as though his hardship is a bundle that he must safeguard with his body. In his good hand, he holds a bottle of acrid amber liquor.

Andra is afraid—for the others, yes, but mostly for herself. Kody's employ has never been more than a meager protection. Soon it will fail entirely. For as long as she's been with him, she's studied the roles that her fellow performers play, both in the Show and outside of it. She has concluded that none of them are what they might, in a better world, have been. She will mourn Jorg. She will mourn them all.

But she has known loss before. What she fears most is the end of the Show—and what comes after. On the last page of her life's script, a man waits. He is beautiful, cunning, and steeped in power. He is both the Empire's finest writer of verse and its most skilled sorcerer. Illness does not trouble him. Age does not touch him. In throne rooms and grand halls, he is called the Light of the Sun. His name is Pol. He is the man who set Andra on her path, and he will be the one who marks its end. She has seen it, just as she has seen Jorg's end.

As long as she has the Show, she will be safe. She has seen that much. But soon Jorg will die and the Show will stagger and fall. When it does, Andra will fall with it.

Grimly, she stares into the fire, earthly avatar of the divine sun, and prays for answers.

All she finds is memory.

II: The Curse

Andra's life began in a nameless desert outpost at the far eastern edge of the Empire of the Sun. According to common understanding, her people were simple, hardy folk who gladly took it upon themselves to act as the vanguard of the Empire's outward expansion. In reality, whatever dreams they may once have had of manifesting the Empire's great destiny, they instead found themselves committed to lives of interminable toil and lack. They had no luxuries to speak of, and the magics they practiced were small and unexceptional. They gnawed ox tendons for strength. They kept small, sun-colored agathodaemons for good luck. To obtain any other needs that their labor could not buy, they prayed.

Yet even in Andra's wasteland town they knew the name Pol. His couplets served as aphorisms. As a game, children claimed his identity and pretended to possess whimsical and implausible powers. Rumor had it that he had the favor of the Emperor himself and that it was the Emperor who had given Pol his honorary title. Having no firsthand experience of such advantages, Andra's people believed all of it. He occupied an entirely different sphere. For him, anything was possible.

So when he arrived among them one day in Andra's twenty-fourth year amid a pack of bodyguards and syco-phants, they wasted no time on disbelief. Visitors to their town were rare; visitors with hangers-on were unheard of. Yet that was neither the only nor the main sign of his identity. Like the true light of the sun, there was something about Pol that made it hard for Andra's neighbors to look at him for more than a fleeting moment or two. That was how they knew whose presence they were in.

He and his cortege bypassed the town's few amenities and made for Andra's hovel directly. Silence followed them like a shadow. She tracked their progress from within her home, listening to their footfalls against the stillness. On the frontier, silence implied inactivity, and inactivity was a comfort that Andra and her neighbors could ill afford. Her windows were shuttered against the harshness of the midday light, so she could not say what was coming. Even so, she knew that she would be tested.

Pol's guards entered first and surveyed the dimmed room for any hidden weapons or other dangers. They wore sheathed shortswords and breastplates embossed with the crest of the sun, and they moved through Andra's home without regard for her person or property. When they were satisfied, one of them went back outside to retrieve Pol while the other fixed himself by the door. Neither had spoken a word.

When Pol entered, Andra almost gasped aloud. She hadn't known that a man could be so lovely. He wore a sleeveless sandstone-colored tunic and light, laurel-green salvars, and he moved as though movement itself were the highest form of decadence and indulgence. The muscles in his forearms were taut, and among his copper ringlets were slender lines of gold that flashed when they caught the muted light. Andra barely noticed the other men who followed him in.

He caught her gaze as he sat across her table, and he held it as he leaned back in his chair.

"Do you know who I am?" he asked in a voice like white silk.

"How could I not?" she replied in the most disinterested tone she could fake. "Surely even the dust of the ground knows enough to recognize the illustrious footsteps of the great Pol."

He answered back quickly, as though that was the response he had expected. "Then surely you know why I've come. I must know if your reputed powers are real."

Andra never considered telling him the truth. Like the rest of her people, she had no abilities beyond those conferred by her hands and her wits. But for years, she had earned her bread by posing as a fortuneteller. Aided by a collection of cheap and useless props—a deck of divining cards, a pile of small bones, parti-colored crystals, and sundry other suggestive contrivances—she gave her people what they needed: reliable advice clothed in fanciful language. In her time she had dispensed simple practicalities for the ignorant, level-headed counsel for lovers and mourners, and sweetened fantasies for those who needed nothing more than a moment of softness and relief.

Most of her neighbors listened and some defied her, but only a few responded as Pol had. Her first reaction to him was disappointment. This was too common a provocation for such an exceptional encounter, this attempt to catch her out. His challenge was every skeptic's demand, a rigged game of hide-and-seek with a peevish child. But after a moment's thought, Andra reconsidered. She looked at him again—his fine clothing, his retinue, the hauteur in his eyes. *All this*, she thought, *just so he can discredit a woman from a town too small to merit a name?* No: He had some vulnerability, some weakness or lack, and somehow he had come to believe that her false foresight could supply him with a remedy. Her heart pounded a warning in her chest. But her curiosity sang stronger and she decided to allow their game to unfold.

"I suppose I should be flattered," she said. "But do

you truly know why you've come? With your fame, your fortune, your powers—why, if even half of what I've heard is true, there must be very little indeed that you can't have. Most of those who pass through my door are afraid of what they might learn of their futures. But what could you have to fear?"

She hoped to mollify him. Instead, he scowled at her as though she'd served him curdled milk.

To stop him from giving voice to his expression, Andra quickly spoke again. "Yet there are some few matters that cannot be solved through ordinary means alone. And so you pursue knowledge of an extraordinary sort."

His manner relaxed slightly, though his displeasure was still not gone from the air. "I banished fear from my life long ago," he says. "But you do have one thing that I need."

At this, the guard who'd remained inside the room shifted his weight from foot to foot. The sound of his equipment settling back in place sent Andra's pulse skittering across her limbs. She willed herself to keep her focus on Pol.

"What we need," she said, "is often very different from what we want. How do you know that you're chasing the right prize?"

A laugh soured in his mouth and his sycophants burbled quietly to each other. "How do I know? Because I am not a fool. I have no interest in the magics of rule or war or love. Whether hated or admired, all flesh dies. Only words are immortal. Only *my* words. I've eaten the voice box of the lyrebird so that all the world's music would live in my verse. I've drunk the blood of a wood frog so that I might see the frozen deadlands of the south with my own eyes and write of what I saw. I've breathed in the powdered bones of the bradán feasa so that every line could shine light on the hidden truths that lurk in men's hearts. No living poet can match my virtuosity, and, so long as I live, I will ensure that no one ever does.

"Yet even if I should find some magic by which to preserve my youth, how can I be sure that death will never find me? The hazards of this world are too varied and persistent to be circumvented by luck alone. A greater power is required."

Andra nodded gravely. "And so you've come here, to me, to seek the source of my sight. But you've come in vain."

Pol tensed in his seat. Around him, the room faded. As it did, his every color flared, as though all the world's light was drawn to him alone. He seemed to gather into himself an authority that would nullify all else: not only Andra and her threadbare stagecraft but even the syrupy adulation of his followers and the latent violence of the armed guard behind him. A sudden heat blanketed Andra and prickled her eyes. Her head spun. Through her confusion, Pol spoke slowly, with a threat in his voice, "Have I really?"

Panic broke over Andra like a sunrise. Either through magic or some monstrous strength of conviction, Pol's will was heavenly in its heft and its wrath. Caught in its blaze, Andra felt her resolve burn away. She wanted nothing more than to give the mage what he asked for. She craved his satisfaction. But not even Pol could overwhelm the truth. Once more, she forced her voice to be calm.

"You want to know my secret," she said. "Very well. You won't be the first to know, and you won't be the last. But your knowledge will only frustrate you the more. There are some things that must lay forever outside the human grasp. This is one.

"As a child, I wandered away one day and lost myself in the brittle scrub. I quickly became thirsty, but it hadn't rained for months and I had no way of finding water. Droughts are common here. They start without warning, and we have no way to know when they'll end. I suppose they're the price we pay for the Empire's expansion. I knew about them, and I knew their danger. But," she said, and shrugged, "I was a child."

Had she faltered in the presentation of her story, Pol's presence would have shaken her hold on it. But it was a tale she'd told many times before, and it had become an easy and practiced accounting. What's more, she had absolute faith in it, because she knew with certainty that not a word of it was true. "As night fell, I curled on the ground, fearing an isolated death. Somehow I must have slept, because the sound of buzzing woke me. It was still well before dawn and my throat felt like old paper. But I stood and followed the sound, not even knowing why.

"What I found was a beehive peeking out from the ground. I had never seen such a thing—as you might imagine, our land is not hospitable to creatures whose lives rely on things as fragile as flowers. Yet there the hive was, buried in the dirt.

"Only, the bees were leaving. As I watched, the entire swarm poured out of its hive and began to fly west, towards the rising moon. I was grateful—and desperate. I didn't even wait until they were all gone. I reached into their hive, felt the last traces of their honey, and took as much of the comb as I could. Some of it I ate then and there. It wasn't much, but it gave me the strength to follow them. The rest I carried with me in my hands."

She paused to ensure that Pol still believed her. When she saw that he did, she continued. "We traveled until dawn, then they burrowed back into the ground. We slept, woke at nightfall, and travelled again. We did this for three days as I slowly ate the last of the honeycomb. Finally, on the evening of the fourth day, it rained.

"It was only a small storm, an hour at most. But it was enough for the plants around us to rouse and blossom. When they did, the bees were ready. They worked with an incredible intensity through the day and into the next, both to harvest the pollen and to build their new nest. I sipped rainwater from cupped blossoms and watched.

"That night, while I slept, I had my first vision of the future. I saw my parents searching for me, holding out hope against hope. And, somehow, I knew that it wasn't a dream, that it was showing me exactly when and where they would be. The next day, I nearly ran there. I was delirious when they found me—scorched by the sun and sapped by hunger. It was only after I recovered that I realized what had happened. The bees knew that the rain would come days before it did. They even knew where it would fall most heavily. That's how they survived. Like other desert creatures, they traveled from storm to storm. But instead of waiting until after the rain and then racing against time, they moved only when they knew that the flowers would be there, waiting for them. And because I ate their honey—"

"You gained their power," Pol said. He leaned back in his chair, and the sense of his untouchable superiority waned. "So, all that remains is for you to take me to them. That shouldn't be too difficult, should it?"

But Andra had designed her story just so she could brush off such attempts at manipulation. "You seem to forget," she said, "that the hive is nomadic. Even if it wasn't, I was a child then. I have no memory of where I was or how to return there. You're free to search the desert for as long as your stamina allows, but I can be of no further help to you."

Pol waved this away as if he had expected it. "Yes, they migrate, making their location impossible to guess. But you don't need to guess. You're a seer. Just use your power to see where they'll be tomorrow, and our business will be done."

"The visions aren't mine to control. Not even for one such as you."

A moment passed. Pol waited for Andra's will to break. He waited in vain.

Then, slowly, he said, "'One such as you.' You must think you know me. Allow me to assure you that you do not."

Within an eyeblink, he had a hand on her throat. His face loomed in Andra's left eye. In her right, his chair clattered against the wall and fell to the floor.

"Do you know," he asked calmly, "the origin of the word 'snakebit'? There's a species—a cousin, actually, of the agathodaemons that you keep—known as the cacodaemon. Whereas your little pets bring good luck, the cacodaemon brings bad luck. That is, its venom carries a curse. Because of this, the cacodaemon is loathed in equal measure as your agathodaemons are loved. They're considered evil, and most people would kill a cacodaemon on sight. But most people are fools, because power makes no distinction between blessing and curse."

While his left hand retained its grip on her throat, he held his right palm in front of her face. She saw a snake tattooed there in the shape of a spiral. "This ink is mixed with the venom of a cacodaemon. The power that it confers is the power to lay curses." He placed that hand on her cheek, then spoke again. "Now, will you tell me where to find the honey that grants the power of future sight?"

Andra's mind turned blank-white with terror. She would have told him everything, but there was nothing to tell.

Interpreting her silence as refusal, Pol looked at her with something like respect. "I see," he said. "I can't say that I approve of your choice, but I do understand it. Power shared is power lessened. But you'll have the rest of your life to learn that lessened power is better than none at all."

He gripped her skull with his tattooed right hand. The whorling shape of it burned slick against her skin. In all the years later, Andra would remember that when he spoke, his voice was unchanged. She had expected the spell to ring out like a bell or to sough like scales over sand. But it was only her own trickery that relied on such paltry theatrics. Pol's power was entirely real. It was its own announcement.

"No more," he said to her, with one hand still holding her neck and the other leeching magic into her, "no more will you gain the benefits of your foresight. From now on, you will be known as a liar by all. Neither strangers nor your neighbors nor even your own flesh and blood will credit your visions. All of your warnings and guidance will fall on deaf ears. This will be your curse for the rest of your days."

Then the magic in his tattoo faded and he released her. As a piercing blur descended over her vision, she looked up at him with a question in her eyes. Yet he suddenly seemed to be no more aware of her than the sun is aware of those who pray for shade. Underneath the dancing, pitiless glare of the curse, she felt a part of herself bend and collapse. She was unconscious before Pol reached the door.

III: KOBOLD KODY

The morning after her vision, Andra takes a walk in the woods near the Show's encampment. Even now, in her old age, large congregations of trees are alien to her. Her instincts and feelings are still those of the girl who watched her elders wrest an entire settlement from a barren landscape that offered scant help and that parceled out only the most meager of rewards. For all in her life that has changed, Andra still carries her home in her heart. It makes her out of place in the constant, kaleidoscopic shifting and unfolding of the forest. After only a short while, she decides she's seen enough.

It's no wonder that faeries prefer these places, she thinks ruefully as she makes her way back over roots and fallen logs, *a forest is half a mischief all on its own*. It is also beautiful, she would admit, and beguiling, and rich in vitality. But Andra has never sought mischief.

Waiting for her at the border of the woods is Kody, the Show's captain and namesake. Out of costume, he appears more or less like any other working man. He is darkened from his years in the sun, and he wears scuffed leather boots, dark pants, a tan shirt, and a goatee that he keeps just a bit too long. Thanks to an old war wound that the showman habitually plays up as part of his act, he always stands at a slight tilt. In the Show, when he stands under the lights in his brightly embellished soldier's uniform and his stage makeup, he seems almost unearthly, not merely the human leader of the circus but its very spirit. In the privacy of the camp, it's easier to see that he is older in his heart than his body will ever be.

Andra more closely resembles her role. Her desert upbringing has left her gaunt and hard-eyed, and age has thinned and grayed her hair. Her sleeves are long and loose, and under them her skin is pale. She needs no costume: One look alone is enough to mark her as a mystical recluse whose gaze pierces the veil of time.

At the moment, however, the uneven forest floor has played one too many tricks on her and she is laboring to see past her next few steps. She barely registers Kody's presence and almost passes him by before he says, "Why, hello, Andra—I wouldn't have expected to find you here. Checking up on something you've seen?"

Andra isn't ready to mention Jorg. She shakes her head and waits until her breathing has slowed enough to answer, "Just taking a walk."

Kody pats her amiably on the shoulder and nods. "Good. A little unexpected excitement every now and then can be welcome, but as a rule I do so prefer for our time on the road to be as uneventful as possible. You will let me know if there are any obstacles in our path, won't you?"

She nods absently. There's nothing she can do to control what she sees. Only others can act against her visions, and only Kody has ever believed her enough to try. Now that she's had a moment to gather herself, the light-headedness from her walk fades into hunger, and she follows the campfire smells and cooking sounds that are coming from inside the ring of the Show's brightly painted wood-and-canvas wagons. But before she leaves Kody altogether, she turns to him and asks, "If you knew that one of us was better off outside the Show than in it, would you still keep them here?"

Kody straightens himself slightly. "Somebody like who, exactly? Don't tell me that you're thinking of leaving us. Andra, dearest Andra, you'd tell me if anything was wrong, wouldn't you? We've been in this together for far too long not to be honest with one another."

She hesitates. She remembers the blood on Jorg's hand, his motionless body on the ground. For the space of a breath she wants to tell Kody what she's foreseen. He approaches as though to reassure her, but she knows by his gait and by the new softness in his eyes that whatever he says next will be salesmanship dressed as sympathy. She feels her heartbeat at the base of her throat and fights the urge to let him speak first. "Honesty, then: Would you send one of us away for our own sake? Or would you keep us here for yours?"

In the half-a-heartbeat before Kody answers, Andra watches him pass through all the stages of constructing and then issuing a lie. His eyes unfocus while he calculates the meaning of her question. Then, having assured himself of the fact that her question is no mere hypothetical, he begins to smile. He has two courses open to him, both of which will be easier if he stays on friendly ground. Either he'll worm the truth out of her or he'll dissemble in the hopes that she'll believe him until it's too late. Settling on the latter, he finishes by rearranging his expression into the very picture of selfless solicitude and says, "Why, Andra, more than any of the others, you and I know how hard a place the world can be. I would never knowingly make it harder. But my policy has never changed. Anybody who finds a better life is welcome to it—entirely welcome! Why would I want to keep someone on who didn't want to work with me? I am but a humble citizen of the Empire, and as such I hold that every man under the sun is free to choose for himself. I would never try to force anyone into my employ, nor would I try to force them out."

It's a sound act, well-constructed and bearing every recognizable mark of sincerity. But Andra has seen it far too many times over the years to be taken in. She thinks of Jorg and tilts her head down and away from Kody so that her graying hair blocks him from her view. "Well, then," she says, "I suppose I have my answer. But I'll thank you to tell me directly next time and save your palaver for the paying customers."

She turns towards a gap in the wagons, but behind her she hears Kody laugh off her barb. "Do you know what the best part of being a showman is?" he asks lightly. "Anybody who calls you a liar is just accusing you of doing your job."

★★★

Despite all her years under his employ, Andra can say very little with certainty about the man who calls himself Kobold Kody. Both onstage and off, he advertises himself as a former officer in the Imperial army. She knows that he is not. The most obvious tell is the fact that he sometimes changes his supposed rank: captain one day, colonel the next. Having worked his Show for so long, Andra also knows that the insignia he wears on his costume are not his. She was there the night he received them.

It was in the Show's early days, when they still played next to campfires under the open sky. The original owner of the military honors was a man with a proud bearing and a weight on his heart. Even in the inconstant firelight, Andra knew the cause as soon as she saw him: love.

Evidently Kody knew as well. As Andra watched through the milling crowd, he approached the heartsore veteran and struck up a conversation. Within a minute, Kody had pulled a small green bottle from the inside of his coat. Like all of his fraudulent potions, it bore no label, allowing Kody to tailor its alleged effects to his mark's need. The veteran looked at the bottle. He looked at Kody. He looked back at the bottle, this time with money in his hand.

But Kody knew what he wanted. Feigning romanticism, he pushed the man's hand away. The ensuing negotiation was no less scripted than any of Kody's other acts, though only one of the two participants knew it. In the end, the veteran had the phony love tonic and the showman had the authentic insignia. From where Andra stood, it was hard to say who was more pleased.

Yet somehow she has always sensed that Kody is more than a shameless swindler. Though he freely embellishes his past, he has a soldier's wary eye for danger. He knows how to track and hunt. And sometimes, when the Show has had more than its share of good or bad fortune, he joins his cast and crew at their campfire and tells stories that Andra cannot fully discount.

When his spirits are high, he tells of the land as it was before the Empire's expansion, of goblins and orcs prowling wild countries under open skies. When the Show falls on hard times, he speaks of the butchery and bloodshed of war. In his actorly telling, he lacquers these tales until they take on the glowing grandeur of myth. If pressed, he will swear to the absolute veracity of every particular, just as a shopkeeper will vouch for the integrity of even his flimsiest wares. Yet like a dusty heirloom that has been restored to its original luster, Kody's narratives are materially sound underneath the layers of varnish he applies to them.

In Andra's experience, there has only been one occasion on which he allowed the truth about himself to be seen in an unrefined state. After a performance one night in some outlying hamlet, a customer approached him to ask if she could join the Show. This was no rare event. No more than half of the Show's population were recruited; the other half joined on their own initiative. Under normal circumstances, Kody would briefly interview the aspiring performer in order to ascertain their ability and temperament. But on this night, the applicant led the interview herself.

She had black hair and eyes hard enough to give her an authority beyond her years. She introduced herself as Zula. "I'm a fireshaper," she said. Then she proceeded to demonstrate, instantly wreathing herself in flame without suffering either injury or discomfort. "I'm looking for a suitable platform for my skills," she said, still clothed in fire. "Your Show is a little worse for the wear, but it has its appeal. Tell me why I shouldn't wait for something better." Only then did she allow her fire to go out.

Perhaps it was the challenge that broke Kody out of his regular habit of partial honesty. Perhaps he was desperate to win such an unequivocal talent, or perhaps he was simply tired. Whatever the reason, he explained himself in full as Andra and a few others watched.

"You ask that question like you think you're free," he said. "Free to wait, free to choose. But I can tell you with full confidence that you are not. Your magic is impressive, I confess. Yet as much as I admire your resourcefulness, you don't know how much trouble you're about to get yourself into.

"Before your time, magic was like any other part of nature. If people used it at all, they used it to live—and if they didn't use it, they weren't all that much worse off. But that's not how the Empire sees things. Imperial magic is like nothing you can imagine. In the capital, they treat it like grain or silver, like something to be weighed, measured, and parceled out only to those who have something to give in exchange. Here, you're all just people —neighbors, family, friends. But it won't be that way for long. In the Empire, there are only two kinds of people: the ones who are rich in the right kind of magic and the ones who aren't."

A curl of pride licked across Zula's face. But Kody wasn't done. "You think you're safe just because you have a little power. You're not. The Empire may not reach out a generous hand to those who are poor in magic, but it does tolerate them. The same can't be said for those who it sees as competition. As soon as they find out that you have something that you didn't ask them for first, they'll hunt you down like you were a counterfeiter. But don't take my word for it. Ask a barbarian—if you can still find one. Ask a goblin or an orc. They all had their own kind of power, just like you do now. And the Empire wiped them all off the map."

Then, for the first time in their conversation, he turned away from Zula and acknowledged their ragtag audience. "No one here has a place in the world the Empire is building. Those people in the capital only know one story, and if you don't fit inside that story they will eat you alive. That's why you need my Show. Anyone who shows the Empire something it doesn't expect is liable to get torn apart. But if you put on a good enough act, then you can do anything you want behind the curtain.

"I wish I could give you the power to change the story we're all living in," he continued somberly. "But I can't. The most I can do is help you change *your* story." He waited for Zula to meet his eye, then spread his hands. "Take it or leave it."

By then, Andra had heard him give any number of recruitment speeches. But none of them was as full or direct as the one he gave to the young fire mage. It worked, as Andra knew it would. Zula joined them that very night, leaving her home without even pausing to say her goodbyes.

IV: Blade, Box, Scale, Shard

After her brief interchange with Kody, Andra chooses to eat her breakfast with the members of the sideshow: Harold, the World's Tallest Halfling; Coner, the Lizard Man; Lady Ugok, the Civilized Ogress; Etain, the Contortionist; and the Human Pincushion, whose name no one can ever quite bring to mind. She finds them sitting on a spare piece of canvas spread on the ground. As she approaches, a sudden pop sounds from behind one of the wagons. All six of them watch as a thin tail of white smoke rises from the spot.

"One of these days, that girl is going to get herself in trouble," Andra says, shaking her head.

"Well, and good morning!" Harold says.

"I'm sorry," the Pincushion says, turning between his companions and the tapering smoke. "Who's going to get herself in trouble? Should—should we go and check?"

"Ach, it's just Zula," Harold replies. He resumes his breakfast, talking between bits of sausage and bread. "She's always tinkering with her act. No cause for worry there. I'm more interested in what inspired this one to go for a ramble at the first light of day," he adds, gesturing to Andra. "Forests and halflings have never got on too well—it's the short legs, you know."

Andra smiles. His cheeriness is a rare and precious resource among the cast. Harold has good reason to maintain such high spirits: Uniquely among Kody's menagerie, his time with the Show will end in a homecoming. As he has explained to his castmates, halflings believe in seeing something of the world and tasting its foreignness before settling into their traditional ways of life. For him, the Show is merely a vehicle for such experimentation. Andra finds his company to be genuinely pleasant, and she does not hold it against him that she herself has no such place of return.

"Well," she answers, "long or short, all legs need to be stretched every now and again. I thought I'd do mine this morning."

Harold nods approvingly. "Ah, how lovely. Forests notwithstanding, we halflings are a walking people, you know. There's a saying we have, that the intelligent man thinks with his head but the wise man thinks with his feet."

Coner snorts at this through his slit nostrils, but he says nothing.

"Well," Harold says, making it a point to look at Andra, "it's a habit that I enjoy, anyway. Always seem to find the thoughts that I'm looking for, when I'm walking."

"And what about the thoughts you want to lose? Can you walk them to exhaustion as well, or do you find that they exhaust you first?" Coner asks. He was born human and became a monster only through his own recklessness. As a child, he was taken by the image of a lizard that climbed the walls of his house and clung to its ceilings. He caught this lizard and ate its legs, hoping to win its powers for himself. Instead, his skin turned to scales and his tongue forked, and he was cast out even by his own parents. Andra imagines that he has many thoughts that he would like to leave behind.

Nor is he the only one. Andra knows that most of the sideshow freaks—most of the Show outright—have wounds or humiliations that they would rather never think on again. Lady Ugok, to Andra's right, entertains passersby by wearing a hoop skirt and petticoats, sitting demurely at a small table, and serving herself high tea. To Andra's left is Kody's new Human Pincushion, a man with trusting eyes who never talks of his past life. In between Harold and Coner is Etain, who sits hunched and rigid, silently rubbing a thumb over the deep-black piece of tile or stone that she wears around her neck as a good-luck charm.

Rather than indulge Coner's bitterness and upset Etain further, Andra brings the conversation back to herself. "As it happens," she says, "I was hoping to find a plan, but it eluded me. Maybe one of you knows where it's hiding?"

Etain takes this as her best chance to help lighten the mood. "What plan would that be?" she asks, looking out from underneath her slanting haircut.

"A plan," Andra answers, "to make Kody do something that he doesn't want to do." That stumps them. With the exception of the Pincushion, they've all been in the Show long enough to know that arguing with Kody is no more useful than pushing against the wind: If he doesn't bowl them over outright, he'll simply go around and reach the same place despite them.

Ever the optimist, Harold speaks first. "Is it something you can effect on your own, this plan?"

Andra shakes her head while she takes a bite of her oatmeal, then says, "No, I'm afraid not."

Warily, the Pincushion speaks up. "But why go against Mister Kody at all? He's the one who's looking after us, you know. He knows what's best."

"He's got his wits about him, that much is for sure," Andra says, an agreement to smooth the path for what comes next. "But he's hardly infallible, is he? And remember," she says with a portent in her voice, "I know what will come to pass."

She sees the Pincushion waver back and forth between rejecting the discomfiting truth that she has told and dismissing it as an overdone posture. It took her years to accept that those are the only two choices she can offer in her cursed condition. It took even longer for her to master the art of walking the line between them. Once she realized what Pol had done to her, she tried to hide her foresight altogether. Then the hiding itself was what people noticed, and that was no better. Over time she learned to hide herself in a showy way, as the architect of a hall of mirrors hides its exit in plain sight. These were hard lessons, and she had no choice but to learn them well.

"I guess I don't know if I believe all that," the Human Pincushion says, "but I'd like to help if I can."

Andra thinks again of the blood on Jorg's hand and looks away. "Thank you. But if it goes as I fear it will, I wouldn't want any of you to be involved."

"Maybe it won't be so bad, whatever it is you're planning for?" Etain asks hopefully. "Maybe it'll all work out?"

Coner snorts again. "If I know anything about Kody, it'll work out for *him* just fine."

Ignoring Coner, Harold places his chin in his hand and says, "Hmm. Well, maybe there really is nothing that any of us can do to change his mind. We all know how Kody can be about his own decisions. But even so, I don't see any reason for despair. As we halflings often say, 'The berries at your feet on the pathside may not fill your belly, but they'll do a good sight better than the roast on the table back home.'" He turns back to Andra. "That is to say, even if the perfect thing is out of your reach, there's always something that'll do in a pinch."

"And if that fails," Coner adds sourly, "you can always just do what Kody himself always does: Fake it until it's too late for your audience to get their money back."

Andra almost ignores Coner's reflexive cynicism. But there is something in it that melds with Harold's advice and adheres in her mind. She chews thoughtfully for a moment or two, but the answer remains just out of reach. When she's done, she places her spoon in her empty clay bowl and stands. "Thank you—both of you," she says. "I'll give this more thought, but you may just be right."

***

Within a few days, the Show caravan arrives outside the walls of the Imperial capital. Andra holds a stack of advertisements in her hands: the dragon-tamer, the pyromancer, the barbarian, the freaks, the goblins, the soothsayer, the ringmaster. Each has been hand-painted and lettered by Lady Ugok, who can neither speak nor understand their spoken languages but whose work with a brush possesses an aching beauty. More than once, Andra has held Ugok's portrait of her and sorrowed that she did not more closely resemble the woman on the paper. In Ugok's hands, Andra cuts an imposing and self-assured figure. The woman herself has been neither of those things since the day that Pol took her life from her.

Andra carries the fliers past the western entrance, the Sunset Gate, and into the city. Once through she finds herself in the workers' quarter, which occupies the lowest-lying area of the city. She is appalled by what she finds there. Andra has a lifetime's worth of experience with want and hardship, but the workers' district in the capital represents a different type of destitution altogether.

At first glance, it is little more than a slum. The homes are ill-constructed and in poor repair. The people carry themselves in postures of spite and misery. Yet as she posts her fliers along the bent and airless alleyways that serve as streets, Andra notices that many of the workers bear odd and mismatched signifiers of wealth: a single article of clothing or jewelry that stands apart; or a rare bird on a string; or some other such trifle. Something, she feels, has been imposed on these people, but she is not sure whether it is their poverty, their evident revulsion at their own station, or something else altogether.

Jorg, she knows, comes from the capital. Now that she has seen it for herself, his drinking is less surprising, though no less saddening. She thinks about him and about the advice given to her by Harold and Coner. She has never been able to reverse any of her visions; that part of Pol's curse has always held true. But neither has she attempted to cheat nor hoax them. This has always been Kody's specialty, the design of clever deceptions. *But if it will save a life*, Andra thinks as she pastes handbills to the uneven stone walls of the workers' hovels, *I'm willing to try.*

This thought leads to another, a memory of a different vision: an elegant tent set upon soft sand, a golden sunset over the water, four powerful artifacts arrayed on a table or chest. Andra loses herself to a familiar fear for an instant and then banishes the image from her mind. The thought of saving Jorg has given this memory, this vision, a new aftertaste. There is hope in it now, and it is the hope, not the fear, that unsettles her the most.

By the time she returns to the carnival site, the sun is setting and the rickety, dust-covered caravan is reassembling itself into something altogether more enticing. The goblins seem to be everywhere at once: extracting props from the wagons, constructing the ticket booth, and pitching the tents, doing everything that elevates the Show from an abnormality to an attraction. Andra steps only where she won't be in their way. She sees the nervous energy of the cast and crew in their rapid movements and their widened eyes. She hears it in their voices. It's strange and giddy and a little bit frightening, this feeling of being a part of something that hungers for its own creation and whose hunger only grows the closer it comes to completion. It's a feeling that Andra cannot now indulge. She is going to see Kody. She has to ask him one more time.

She finds him at the back of the site, looking up at the bold moon. There is a sense of peace around him, as though some invisible wall in the air stops the torchlight and the construction sounds from fully reaching them. "Hello, Kody," she says. "Care to share your thoughts?"

He looks like he wants to give her a light, easy laugh, but instead he looks back towards the dimming sky. "It's been a long road, hasn't it?" He raises his head and nods towards the circus grounds. "There were times I didn't think we'd ever make it this far—traveling the Empire, earning our living and our reputations, boasting so many outstanding acts. It's grown so much, my little Show. I guess I was just thinking about how much bigger it can get." He turns to smile at her. "Maybe next time we're here we'll play in the Imperial palace itself."

Andra nods and says nothing. She allows a moment to pass before she asks, as though the thought has just entered her mind, "Do you remember when you found me?"

"Of course." Kody nods, and then he nods again. "Of course—I remember everyone. Glyn was an orphan, Jorg was at the bottom of a bottle, Harold—well, Harold found me. Anyways, you were back in that little speck town of yours. As I recall you were in a bit of trouble." He chuckles to himself. "I remember thinking you'd probably never been in trouble before. When I walked into your shop, you gave me a look like I was a cruelty that had been sent your way, like a drawing of a loaf of bread that had been handed to a starving man."

Andra smiles. "Well, I never thought that you'd believe a word I said. What use would you have for a seer who no one would believe?"

"A good enough liar can always find a home," Kody says, laughing. "But that's the thing I never understood: You weren't lying. You don't ever lie, and it's a good thing, too, because half of what you say sounds like nonsense. And yet most of those people in your town wouldn't've pissed on you if you were on fire. Why didn't they trust you? I've seen jealousy before, but your gift could've really helped those people."

Andra forces herself to hold his eyes as though the question is a matter of no great importance to her. If she lets on how much the past still hurts he may try to change the subject, and she can't have that. Behind them, there's an exhausted, elated cheer as the bigtop goes up. Andra waits until the quiet returns and then says, "It still can help people."

"Sure can," Kody says. "It helps me every night we sell tickets."

Andra is not in a joking frame of mind. "Don't let Jorg perform. Make him a roustabout if he likes, or expel him from the Show if he doesn't. But don't let him go on anymore."

Suddenly, Kody's eyes turn knife-sharp. "Correct me if I'm mistaken, but I seem to recall us having this conversation already. But just to be sure, I'll ask again: Is this Jorg's request that he's making of his own free will?"

Andra shakes her head.

"Then will it be his idea in the future?"

"No," Andra says quietly, "nothing like that."

"Have you told him yourself that he'll be in danger if

he goes on tonight?"

Andra resents the question for what it forces her to admit. "I don't know that it's tonight. I don't know when it'll be."

In the growing dark, Kody gives her a measured look. "Then why don't you just leave it to me?" he says slowly. "We're family here, Andra. My Show is a home for people who don't have one. I saw enough derelicts when we were at war out on the frontier. I don't need to see more, let alone make 'em. I can't send Jorg away because of something that might not happen for who knows how many years. I need to be there for him—just like I am for you."

Andra hears his message: she has only what Kody chooses to give her, and she should always remember who owes favors to whom. So she does not tell Kody that he is as good as killing Jorg himself. She does not say that the Show is no real home; that a real family doesn't gather its weakest members and call them freaks and put them on display for the entertainment of the jeering public. None of that would change Kody's mind about anything but Andra herself.

For a moment they both stand and say nothing. Ahead of them is full night, and the horizon is visible only as the place where the stars end. Behind them, the Show spreads under enough firelight to provide a false, dancing day.

Then the moment passes and Kody thanks Andra for speaking her mind. "I know you're just trying to do the right thing," he says. "I do still believe you. I just hope you can believe in me, too." He tips his hat to her and is gone, back into the clamor and disruption of his dream assembling itself once more.

Andra will follow him. For the moment, she has no other choice. Before she does, she breathes the night air and thinks back to her first vision.

Pol and his retinue had left her unconscious on the floor, but in her mind she was still with him. They sat together on a pale beach in a tent that was furnished with fine rugs and a cot and chairs made from spruce and pine. As the sun set, the ocean sighed and they talked together for a time. Yet despite the placidity that surrounded them, their conversation quickly grew hostile and they soon fought one another using powerful magics until one of them had ruined the other completely.

Perhaps because she believed it at first to be a simple nightmare, Andra remembers few of the details of this vision. She cannot recall what she and Pol discussed. Nor can she remember how they fought, nor which of them emerged the victor. The tent remains in her memory from the shock of seeing it again when Kody bought it for himself. Andra fears it now, as she knows what it augurs for her future. Still, she knows that she cannot overturn what she has seen. All she can do is prepare such mitigations as she can devise.

But there is one other thing she remembers. In her battle with Pol, she had four weapons at her disposal. They were arrayed in front of her while she and Pol spoke. Andra's memory of them is wavering and suggestive—she has only the vaguest impression of what they might have been. She has come to think of them as the blade of a dragon-slayer, a box of fire, the scale of a nameless creature from deep below the earth, and a shard of petrified lightning.

These images terrified Andra when she first saw them, and they frighten her still. She is no warrior and she has no love of bloodshed. Even with weaponry at hand and her own life at stake, she knows she will be incapable of killing Pol. What she needs, she believes, is an ally, someone who will help her to do the impossible and escape her rendezvous with Pol—or, if her destiny cannot be escaped, to protect her when it arrives. For years, she had hoped that this protector might be Kody. Now, however, Andra finally understands: Kody will not help Jorg, and he will not help her either. Whether she is able to or not, she will have to face Pol on her own.

THE DRAGON-TAMER

I: An Hourglass; A Sacrifice

Jorg wakes with the rising sun, symbol of rising life and holy purity. It isn't the light that has woken him, though. He's awake because the alcohol that put him to bed is finally leaving him. Jorg's life is an inversion, an hourglass in which the sands flow upward, never to find rest. When he reaches for his flask, he finds Andra instead.

"Ah, the seeress," he says. "Go away."

"And a good morning to you," she replies.

He rubs a hand over his face. "If this is your way of making friends, it's no wonder you have so few. Now go away."

When he sees that Andra won't comply, Jorg tries to raise himself to a dignified, seated position. He mostly succeeds. Still, his hair and clothes are wild and unkempt, his posture is sloped, and his blue eyes sharpen with pain as a headache takes hold. He looks up, and the sympathy that he sees in Andra's face stings him even more sharply than his hangover.

She says, "Please listen, Jorg. I've had a vision. Of you."

He grunts and leans forward, pushing her away so that he can search the floor around his bed.

"This," she says, and holds up the silver flask, glowing in the morning light, "this will kill you."

"And you needed your 'vision' for that?" Jorg tries to spit his derision onto the ground but his mouth is too dry, so instead he coughs a laugh at her. "Funny—everyone else seemed to notice just fine on their own. Etain, Glyn, Zula, Harold, the goblins," he ticks them off on his fingers, "even Kody, though at least he's smart enough to keep me supplied. Now give it back. The one thing I know in this goddamned life is how to handle my drink."

"No, please," Andra says, "you have to listen. I don't mean to judge you."

Jorg reaches inside himself for some trace of pliability or openness, but all his stores are dry. All he finds is thirst, and an ache too old and harsh to name. He stands and snatches the flask from Andra with his good hand and says, "Fine—I can't make you stop talking. But I have to do my job. Let's go. I promise you that I can drink and listen at the same time."

Together they walk out of his tent and into the morning. About them is the scent of grass. Their campground is nearly a mile away from the wall of the capital, but the backlit city rules their view and casts them into shadow. Above the city silhouette the sky is opening into pale blue. The two of them make their way easily through the Show's old and weather-beaten carts on their way to the one that houses the other half of Jorg's act.

"You must believe me," Andra says as they walk. "I saw you finish the flask and then collapse during your act. You vomited blood, and you went still. I saw this, I promise you."

Jorg holds up his left hand, long reduced to its outermost two fingers. "I've been through worse." He pauses at a barrel, places the flask on the ground, and pries open the barrel with his right hand. From it he takes out a long strip of salted fish, which he holds with his mangled left hand while he retrieves the flask with his right. "Take one. It'll save me a trip."

Andra does so and then replaces the lid of the barrel, and they walk again. "Please, Jorg," she says, "if not for yourself than for Cary. He depends on you—we all see it."

Jorg's face twists for a moment. Then he tips back the flask. Neither of them speak again until they find Jorg's animal partner. Still asleep under a large canvas dropcloth, Cary seems like some antiquarian statue, some paradigmatic image of savagery in repose. Even sleeping and blanketed, his muscles are pronounced, his raw strength unequivocal. Uncoiled, the trunk of his body alone is nearly twenty feet long and nine high. When he stands on his hind legs and unfurls his tail and wings, he seems to grow in a way that exceeds the corporeal. As Jorg and Andra draw near, the trainer's scent rouses him, and there is such a rush of affection in his eyes that even the alcohol cannot wholly numb Jorg to it.

Cary ignores his breakfast at first so that he can climb down from his cart and nuzzle his long cheek against Jorg's neck and shoulder. They stand there, the cloth pooled to Cary's side and Jorg's arm wrapped around his neck while the beast tastes the air with his tongue until he's satisfied that his master is real. Andra has never been this close to Cary, and her awe in his presence is a bitterness in the back of Jorg's throat. Cary's silver feather-scales ripple softly as he stretches. Then he huffs and they feel the heat of his breath.

"He's magnificent," Andra says, turning to Jorg.

Jorg nods once but does not meet Andra's gaze. She is right: Cary is magnificent. But Jorg didn't want him to be magnificent. He wanted him to be a dragon.

★★★

It had cost him his home, his conscience, and three years of his life, but Jorg had finally reached his goal. He stood in the cliffside cave, breathing hard. Far below, the sound of the waves whispered up at him from the ocean. The cave floor was wet with rain and the dampness of the earth in that country. Its walls shone in the warm light that reflected off some source that was just behind a dip in the rock.

Jorg was sweating through his shirt despite the cool air. He passed a hand across his brow, wiped it across his chest, and thought of the slow, careful climb down to the cave. Another, harder climb awaited him, he knew. However many treasures the dragon had hoarded, Jorg would have to leave them behind. Even with the climbing tools he'd smithed for himself, he was no mountaineer, and he had no desire to burden himself with unnecessary weight. He had come for a trophy of far greater value than precious metal or stones, one that had never before been claimed: a dragon egg, and the dragonling that lay sleeping inside.

Jorg opened his pack and advanced towards the source of the light. But in the back of the cave he found nothing of gold or gems or other conventional worth. There was only the egg, nestled in a bed of seaweed and brambles. It glowed as though the life inside it were a tiny star. Awash in the golden light, Jorg could not help but to envision a most bountiful return for his efforts.

He had need of such a return; his labors called for it. He'd combed through the libraries of the Imperial Academy until he'd learned everything there was to learn about the dragon. He'd followed the rumors of the flying serpent to the old western forests, dark under thousand-foot canopies and eerie with lilting elfsong. From there he'd traveled to the coast, where he'd seen the beast shine against the gray sky; and he'd tracked her to her home. For days he had foraged mushrooms and nuts, and he'd watched. When he knew her habits and predilections, he'd hunted down a young deer and broken its legs, and he'd dragged it to a clearing. There he'd glazed its fur thickly with poisons, and he'd waited with the sound of the fawn's cries mingling with his own heartbeat in his head until the mother dragon had taken the bait. They were the first two lives that Jorg had ever taken.

He put them out of his mind and bent down to retrieve the egg. It was lighter than he'd expected. Still, his climb back up the cliff face exhausted him. By the time the top was within reach, the rain had changed from a pervasive half-mist to an honest storm. Jorg's hands shook from the grip he maintained on his equipment. One thought carried him through: *I have it.* With every breath and every push of his burning legs: *I have it.*

Thunder shivered out towards the horizon as he pulled himself onto land. A skein of lightning snaked above him, and in its ghost light he saw the mother. Her own blood ran between her teeth and one of her legs was already failing underneath her. Her roar stifled every other sound.

Jorg had no weapon. Even if he had had one, he would have lacked the strength and skill to use it. Even if he had had the skill, his enemy would still have been all but invincible. He put one hand out in unthinking supplication, and the mother charged.

It was instinct alone that tossed him out of her path, and instinct, too, that landed him on his side instead of on his back, where the egg still rested. But even instinct could not save him entirely. In her weakened state the mother slipped as she tried to stop her headlong rush. She could only snap at him as she passed. But as she slid and tumbled off the cliff, she took half his hand with her.

Relief and terror shot through Jorg with such force that he understood the extent of his injury only when he saw the rain-dappled blood coursing down his arm. In the brief minutes before fatigue and blood loss overtook him and he fainted, Jorg tended the wound as best he was able. He woke up the next morning still soaked, still seeping blood, thirsty, sick to his stomach, and light-headed with pain. But when he checked the egg, it was still intact.

The following weeks were alchemical. As Jorg traveled back to the capital and his reward, his grief at the loss of his hand, and hence his old life as a smith, mixed with his exaltation at his triumph and the thought of what his new life would be like. Midway to the capital the egg hatched. Jorg marveled at the child's sunlike coloring, the poise in its diamantine eyes, and the speed with which it grew. Jorg felt that he was on the threshold of his true life. He would finally be transmuted, and all that was dross in him would become sterling and gilded and pure.

He arrived at the Academy with a proud smile and a lively step. Wasting no time, he brought his prize to the department of zoology so that its scholars could confirm his victory and crown him accordingly. He was barely through the filigreed doorway before a pimpled novice intercepted him. "Sir, pets aren't allowed in the department," he said.

Jorg laughed kindly so as to show that he indulged the young man's error. "This is no pet. This is a discovery."

"Your drake?"

Jorg faltered. "My—"

"Ashen drake." The novice pointed at the creature. "Proper name *draconus inferior*, more commonly known as a fool's dragon. Easily discernible from adolescence on by its silver-gray scales. Mistaken by ancient explorers for a true dragon, properly classified nearly a hundred years ago. The ashen drake."

"But it's not—just look at its coloring."

The student sighed and hefted the infant creature and showed Jorg a patch of silver on its belly. "Here, see? Many drakes are born gold, but they all fade as they age." He shrugged. "Try not to feel too bad. It really is a common mistake, especially among amateurs."

Jorg went cold. His ears rang with shame, as though he had been publicly taken by a card sharp or otherwise recruited unwittingly as a stooge in some prearranged act. "I traveled for months," he heard himself say, "as far as the west—"

"The western sea, yes," said the novice, bored. "It's their natural habitat. They prefer the climate—direct sun makes them lazy. That's why they're so weak."

Panic pressed down on Jorg, and he held up his ruined hand as if to indicate that, for reasons of both evidence and fairness, it could not be so. "Weak?"

"As a source for human augmentation, that is," the novice explained, unmoved by the evidence of Jorg's sacrifice. "Of course, there are many animals that have more brute strength than we do. But all magical creaturely gifts descend from the blessings of the sun, which in turn is the gift of the one true god Sol. From this it clearly follows that a cloud-chasing beast such as that," he said, pointing again at Jorg's salvation, "must have very few gifts indeed.

"So, no," he said as he waved Jorg away, "that's not a dragon. I'm sorry about your—well, your—you know. But, well, what were you thinking? We in the Academy have the backing of the entire Empire. Even *we* haven't found a dragon yet—and when we do find one, we won't be foolish enough to send a lone, untrained hobbyist to capture it. I don't mean to be rude, but you really should've known better."

A few hours later, Jorg found himself at the bottom of a bottle. He had gambled his life and lost, and the shock of his defeat stole all his strength from him. Grief, anger, guilt, and fear careened within him like grotesque tumblers on a garish stage. He cursed every drake in the sky and every breath of air he'd taken between the capital and the coast. He knew with a blinding certainty that he was a failure and would never be anything else. The best course of action would be to cut his losses and dispose of the worthless animal he'd brought back with him. But the memories of his first killings turned his stomach. He couldn't bring himself to kill again.

Worst of all was the sure knowledge that the novice was right: Jorg should have known better. This thought set the spinning zoetrope of Jorg's memory whirring, and he watched over and over as his life circled back to its beginnings, always to replay the same mistakes that had set him down the same ruinous path.

In the end, Kody was the one who provided such rescue as could be had. The two met in a disintegrating shack some years after Jorg's journey to the coast. Seeing the drake, Kody introduced himself and offered Jorg a job in the Show. Jorg was drunk, and the dirt was his seat. By then he had been so long without hope that he couldn't conceive of its future existence, let alone embrace its current presence. He refused.

Kody would not be brushed off so easily. He challenged Jorg and beguiled him. He heard Jorg's desolate certainties regarding the world, and he met them with questions about Jorg himself. By then, Jorg no longer trusted himself to answer such questions. He bent to Kody's will.

★★★

Now, with the Show nearly ready for its grand debut outside the capital, Jorg stands near the ticket booth as the zoetrope goes 'round again. The images flash in his mind's eye as he stares at the walls of the city and thinks of what might have been, and bile climbs his throat.

Meanwhile, forty feet behind him, Andra comes upon Etain and Glyn, who plays the role of the barbarian in the dramatic portion of the Show. He and the contortionist are readying the booth from which spun sugar will be sold to the capital's children. Andra pauses to lend a hand, glad for the distraction.

"Hello, you two," she says. "It's a pleasant surprise to see that you're still here. I thought everyone had gone into the city."

"Those who wish to avoid being consumed by temptation are best advised not to enter its house," Glyn answers without facing her.

Etain brushes her hair behind her ear, drops her hand to the charm around her neck, and says, "As for myself, I just don't think I'd like the crowds."

Andra is more intrigued by his answer than by hers. Despite the rumors that were passed about in her hometown, Andra knows very little about Glyn or his people. Outside of his friendship with Etain and his strange harmony with the goblins, with whom he shares his act, Glyn is a man who keeps his own counsel.

Nor is this the only way in which he stands apart. He is head-and-shoulders taller than every other member of the Show, as broad through the chest as a horse, and darker-skinned than most of the humans that they encounter. More than that, he orients himself to the world and moves himself through it in a way that marks him as an outsider, as though he heeds signs or voices that others cannot perceive.

"Is there really nothing you'd want, Glyn?" she asks. "They say that the merchants in the capital sell the most potent enchantments in the whole world."

This time he looks at her, and she sees both weariness and sadness in his eyes. "There was once," he says, "a demon who was sealed in a jar. One day a man found the jar and discovered the demon inside it. Because this man was greedy and weak, he tried to bargain with the demon. 'Give me strength and courage for a day,' he said, 'and I'll set you free.' And so the demon gave the man a day's measure of strength and courage. In exchange, the dishonest man peeled back the lid of the jar only as far as the width of one finger.

"And so it went, with the man returning to the demon to ask for more and more, and the demon slowly biding its time until the jar was fully unsealed. But eventually the man had used the demon's strength so often that he forgot how to use his own. When the demon finally escaped the jar and attacked the man for his treachery, it easily overwhelmed him. Whatever he had won for himself with his borrowed strength, he lost it that day, for the demon tore the life from his body and snapped his bones in its teeth."

Andra's smile is a sympathetic one. "I take it you don't want to become that man." He looks at her for a moment more before turning to look at the capital shining in the midday sun on the low hill. All of it, from its dim and cluttered slums to the manors of the wealthy, had been arranged as though in genuflection before the golden dome of the palace. "I want to live with balance. The people of your Empire want something else."

She nods towards Jorg and says, "What about him? What do you think he wants?"

"I don't think that Jorg knows what he wants," Etain says quietly as she empties a bag of fine sugar into a metal drum. "He's always been so sad. I've never understood it, because that drake loves him. We all know he does. Jorg hardly needs more strength or courage than he already has. I heard that he rescued Cary from his nest all by himself. He found Cary's mother dead at the bottom of a cliff, and he climbed that cliff alone just to make sure her babies would survive. I'd never be able to do anything like that." She shakes her head. "It just doesn't make sense."

The story is new to Andra. It smacks of Kody's theatricality and she mistrusts it. Jorg always looked to her as though he was on the edge of something unspeakable, so she always did her best to stay wide of him. He seems that way still—his posture stiff, his breathing ragged. It looks as though he would enjoy nothing more than to shatter the city's walls and scramble its innards. Andra has to admit that Etain is right about this much: There is something about him that does not fit.

To the audience, Jorg's act is one of daring. But the cast and crew of the Show see it for what it is: a kinship, albeit one that remains unrequited. Some of them suspect that Jorg holds himself apart from the world because he feels himself a fraud, which indeed he is and has always been. Yet despite the perpetual shabbiness of Jorg's affections, his bond with the drake that masquerades as a dragon verges on the preternatural. That bond is strong enough that Zula can create and sustain the pyrotechnics that are necessary to perpetuate the illusion of Cary's dragonhood without the drake lashing out in fear or otherwise breaking character. Those are the moments that tempt his castmates to see the drunken animal trainer in the same way that the chymist sees a lump of dross: as something coarse and base that must still somehow possess the exalted essence of gold.

What the key to his transmutation might be, no one can say, least of all Jorg himself. It certainly cannot be found in the Show. Parading a shameless hoax before a wide-eyed audience may come naturally to a man like Kody, but it makes for harsh and woeful employment for a man whose livelihood depends on a prize that only a fool could have won.

No—Jorg knows that there is no help for him here. He also knows something deeper, something hidden from everyone but himself: that he was a freak long before the blunder that cost him the better part of his hand. That he made himself into a living artifice, a stratagem impersonating a man. That he was, in short, destined for the Show.

He accomplished this by devoting his life to building a forgery of himself, not realizing until it was too late that the forgery would inevitably come to take the place of the original article. Now, as that same counterfeit copy stands in the sun and hears his name passed back and forth behind him, he drinks, he looks at the capital's outer wall, and he remembers—as he always remembers, as he is never strong enough to stop remembering—that, on every count, he is a failure. But he was not always that man.

II: A Tool Specially Fitted

Jorg was born in the capital to parents who smithed white and red metals. They maintained some popularity among the city's tradespeople and merchants for their artistry, but their most significant patron was the Imperial Academy, home to those who studied the magical properties of the world's creatures. From the Academy's hallowed walls, servants and runners would descend on Jorg's parents' shopfront bearing designs for new tools with which to advance the knowledge and glory of the Empire.

Often, those same servants would return to bear the finished item back to its laboratory home, but there were times when Jorg's parents were instructed to deliver the items themselves. Jorg did not participate in these outings as a child. Only in his adolescence, as his parents aged and he grew into himself, did they ask him along. At his first encounter with the Academy, he was fourteen years old, with his father's wavy mahogany hair, his mother's patient eyes, and the smooth muscles and strong hands that they all shared from metalworking.

He and his parents had left their workshop as a family. Jorg had the pride of carrying his parents' latest product, a cloth-wrapped copper retort, through their neighborhood and up the gentle hill towards the Imperial district in the east. As they progressed, the streets widened and the buildings changed. The sharp corners and stonework of the workers' districts gave way, and the rounded, wooden walls of the favored classes took their place. Jorg saw more trees than he ever had before, more trees than he could name, each of them stretching towards the light as if to offer praise to the great solar disk whose image had been adopted as the official insignia of the Empire of the Sun.

The people, too, were different. Jorg's parents comported themselves always with quiet equanimity. Their work absorbed them easily and naturally, and Jorg had learned his own self-assurance from the long, slow language of their breaths and the unhurried blows of their hammers. They wore simple clothes and presented themselves simply, with no affectations. To Jorg, all of this was not only respectable but natural.

The people of the Imperial district changed that. They spoke loudly and gestured with their hands in extravagant, dramatic swoops and arcs. Some of them, who had eaten the oily skin of the chameleon or sipped the bitter melanins of the addax, seemed to be painted in pale curls of russet, olive, thistle, goldenrod, lavender, laterite, and a thousand other shades that shifted with the lingering slowness of a shadow-pattern cast by gently waving leaves. Others wore pendants of stylized suns and rings made of precious woods. Still others walked about with cloud-white caladrius birds perched on their shoulders as wards against illness or, at their heels, antlered Ceryneian hinds, which were said to run faster than an arrow in flight.

By the time the parchment-colored wood towers of the Academy campus came into view, Jorg was too over-awed even to speak, cowed into silence by the opulence of the Imperial quarter. The things he witnessed there disturbed some inner equilibrium of his, and he passed the remainder of that first journey in a daze.

It was only on a later assignment, when he was somewhat older and his parents sent him alone to take an order from a low-ranking tutor, that Jorg's sentiments came to rest in a new shape. The tutor was blond-haired, short, and barely older than Jorg himself. They met in his laboratory. It was a round room, filled with tables on which rested phials, beakers, jars, tongs, gloves, scales, measuring spoons, coal pencils, clamps, and all manner of other purpose-built bric-a-brac. It had no windows and was firelit by a number of chimneyed hearths.

"It's a bit dimmer in here than we'd prefer," the tutor explained as he sat on a stool and gestured for Jorg to do the same, "and we'd rather let in the sun if we could, but we've discovered that solar rays have some inherent power that alters the properties of some substances, thereby interfering with our experiments." He smiled at Jorg in the manner of a neighborhood gossip. "Some of my more, ah, freethinking colleagues propose that this property of sunlight will eventually fall under our chymistry. One day, we'll be able to bend the sun's light and purify it in just the same way that we do metals or salts."

Jorg sat. The idea of lightsmithing struck him as a pure fantasy, an absurdity that defied all reason. Yet everything about the tutor spoke of education and intelligence, whereas everything about Jorg spoke of ignorance. "Is that what you believe?" he asked.

The tutor leaned against a table leisurely. "Oh, no. Our limitations are surely far too pronounced for anything like that. I believe in the holy word and that all of Sol's creations bear his imprint. That's the only reason that our research exists at all: Our god created the whole world in his image, distributing to each creature a mere sample of his own divine potency. The characteristic faculty of the human animal, for example, is the ability to take those powers and claim them for our own. In this way, we are the most godlike of his creations—although, naturally, we can never truly approach his perfection."

Jorg said nothing. He, too, knew the scriptures. His

parents had read them to him as bedtime stories, and he considered them to belong to him and he to them. But the god of those scriptures had always been beyond both contemplation and action. The easy familiarity of the tutor's attitude towards Sol startled Jorg, and he did not respond.

"Well," the tutor said, seeing Jorg's hesitation, "enough preaching. You're here for business, after all, and I don't want to keep you." He showed Jorg a series of glass cylinders that the Academy had recently commissioned from one of the city's glassblowers. He explained that they needed a metal device that could spin those containers at a high and sustained speed. "We're calling it a centrifuge," he said. "We think it might help to distill the humors of the opossum, as the Emperor has asked us to do."

"The opossum?" Jorg asked with no small incredulity. He had seen opossums before. They did not strike him as obvious candidates for Imperial inquiry.

The tutor nodded vigorously. "Yes—the opossum is immune to all known venoms and toxins. The Emperor wisely hopes to acquire a similar immunity. After having made numerous failed attempts to locate the source of this protection, we now believe that it traces to some humor or fluid of the creature's. With the centrifuge, we'll be able to isolate these substances and test them one at a time until we find the right one."

"I didn't know. I thought opossums were just ugly, furry things with sharp teeth."

"Sol's creations truly are wondrous, aren't they," the tutor replied. "We find new gifts everywhere we look— and the more we look, the more we see how much more there is to find."

Jorg knew then that he had found an opening. The Academics, the royalty, the army, the rich—whatever differences in appearance and conduct separated them from him, they did not form a closed circle after all. Even their best minds openly admitted ignorance, and underneath that ignorance was a desire not for some empty token or fashion but for something tangible and real. *If I can find something they haven't*, Jorg thought to himself while the tutor prattled on, *a trophy they can't ignore, I can join them.*

He knew that it might take years to find such a treasure, if indeed one existed at all. He knew also that acquiring such a thing would call for ingenuity and perseverance. But, in his metalworking, he called every day upon his patience, his resourcefulness, his confidence, and his strength. They would carry him through this as well. And by the time he was done, he would have bent himself into a tool specially fitted to pick the locked order of the capital.

III: The Dragon

All day long Jorg stands under the panoptic sky, squints at the capital, and drinks. He empties his flask before the sun touches the horizon. It's still not enough.

When he returns to his quarters for a new bottle, it's not where he remembers leaving it. He thinks of Andra's earlier interference and has a sensation as though of a tarry acid in his chest. *She wouldn't,* he thinks. *It must be here somewhere.*

And it is, albeit fallen somehow underneath his cot. By the time he finds it he has turned the rest of his tent inside out, but the mess doesn't matter. His fresh and glowing sunburn doesn't matter. The capital outside, still as haughty and indomitable as it ever has been, doesn't matter. All that matters is the drink: its reproach, its renewal, its sting. He is still trembling from his frenzied search, and he drinks with an addled and reflexive desperation. And that, finally, is when Andra arrives.

Jorg is on the floor, saturated with drink, sitting amidst a tumble of clothes, ascenders, rescue eights, harnesses, toiletries, hammers, pouches, ropes, and other sundry goods, many of them made dull or brittle by the passage of time. "Are these all yours?" he hears the fortuneteller ask.

Bleary with relief and disgust, he raises his flask. "Yes—and so is this." He thumps his chest. "And this. And if you've come to tell me more of your lies, you may as well just leave now."

Andra finds an empty space on the ground and sits.

"That's not why I'm here. I know that you'll do what you like. And it wasn't a lie—I truly did see your death. You collapsed during a performance, and Cary took your body and flew away." She pauses. "He loves you, you know."

"Love?" Jorg laughs a sideways laugh. "I feed him. He doesn't love me any more than I love Kody."

"Then why are you here, if you have no love for this?"

Suddenly, Jorg is on the brink of weeping. "Why am I here? Why am I here? Why are *you* here, seeress? Why are any of us here? There's nowhere else for me to go. I have nothing else."

"What about all this? What are these for? They don't look like a soldier's tools. Who were you before you were a dragon-tamer?"

"Not a soldier," he says, "Never wanted to be a soldier. Never wanted to kill. I was a smith."

"You mean you made these?" Jorg hears the admiration in her voice and recalls a time when his pride would have chimed with hers. But that part of him corroded away long ago.

"Jorg," Andra continues, "these are extraordinary. How did you learn to do this?"

"M'parents," he mumbles. "Smithed their whole lives. They were the best in the whole capital. It was all they knew. Only red and white—a neighbor taught me the black."

"They sound like good people. What happened between you? Are they still alive?"

Andra reaches out and places a hand on his arm. Her touch is soft, and its softness slips somehow past the clanging parade of errors that endlessly renews itself in his heart, and it weakens him. His arms slump to his sides. His fingers slip down and away from the flask. "I don't know. I left them."

Softer even than Andra's touch is her voice. "So why not go back? We're right here. Kody won't stop you."

Even though it's only a question, he feels that she has read his mind. He has been picturing it all day long: not just a return but a rebirth, a full and flawless restoration of the blood tie that was the first casualty in his life's misguided crusade. In this reverie, he neither fights against nor runs from the drab and grounded commonality into which he was born. Rather, he embraces it and thrives, for although the tree stretches itself handsomely towards the sacred sun while the stone remains indifferent and inert, the stone is neither broken by the wind nor uprooted by the rain.

But then at some near distance Jorg hears the capering whistle of the barrel organ and the thump of the Show's grand-opening fireworks, and he comes back to himself, back to Andra, back to his flask and the mountaineering equipment strewn about the ground. He comes back to his life, which is neither a tree nor even a stone but a mere handful of sand. He drinks and says, "Back? No. None of us can go back. It's forward or nothing. The Show must go on."

And then Jorg is gone, brushing past her into the dancing dark.

★★★

In Jorg's youngest childhood, in the unknowing purity before the tutor and the drake and the Show, he admired his parents dearly. He had good reason to do so, for the beauty of their work was evident to him even before he had gained the concepts with which to describe it. In seeing how they changed their materials and how their materials in turn changed them, Jorg witnessed something deep and true: in the ash that smeared their arms and foreheads, the fires that kinked and singed their hairs, their sweat, their breath, and the way their hands knew both how to strike and how to shape.

On his initial journey to the Imperial quarter, Jorg came into the presence of shame for the first time, and it pierced him through and through before he even knew how to marshal his defenses. It was the esteem with which the wealthy held themselves; it was the awareness that their esteem was both safehoused in and certified by luxuries that Jorg himself would not have been able to conceive of, had he not witnessed them firsthand. Yet even those splendors and fineries would have weighed only lightly on Jorg if the eyes of the strangers who bore them had been kinder. Those socialites and aristocrats barely glanced at him and his family, but those glances revealed their thoughts well enough. They saw him as a thick-fingered, slow-witted menial. They believed his parents too coarse to clean their own faces.

As Jorg and his family approached the blade-shaped pineboard spires of the Academy, he felt his true and dig-nified self wither under the distorted caricature that had been cast upon him. Like a soft metal, he was stamped by its grotesque weight.

His parents, mere feet away, held firm in the belief that the fads and fancies of the rich came, danced, and faded with all the superficial impermanence of the play of light and shadow on stone. That was their defense, and it carried them through unharmed. But Jorg was open, and the Imperial quarter rewarded his openness by erecting a carnival mirror in his heart, one whose trick image, a misshapen lampoon of himself, would haunt him daily.

Jorg didn't know which treasure he was looking for when he embarked upon his plan to ascend through the capital's ranks. His first thought was to find some clue among the Academics whom he and his family served. Yet, as he grew into full maturity and his association with the Academy deepened, Jorg learned that its public reputation for acuity disguised a private world of speculation, error, and dissension. The scholars and researchers believed to a man that they were gifted with an untouchable genius, yet they all gossiped viciously about each other's flaws and openly scorned each other's labors. They did not agree about which magics were possible or which creatures of legend were real. Half the time they spoke with an erudition that seemed to exceed the human; the other half of the time they spouted vagueries and apothegms that seemed more designed to conceal the truth than bare it. Meanwhile, Jorg's own inquiries were met with ill-disguised disinterest or else were dismissed outright. So, in the end, Jorg was left to gather the necessary information himself.

If anyone mistrusted the presence of a lowly smith in the Academic libraries, nevertheless they allowed him to read undisturbed. As he read he learned of all manner of wondrous creatures: a flaming bird that never died, an insect that walked on water, a lizard whose glance turned its enemies to stone, a fish that summoned lightning. But Jorg had no need for curiosities or amusements. He needed a revolution. There was only one creature that had eluded Imperial science and that was storied enough that it would suffice: the dragon.

One ancient manuscript, illuminated in gold and crimson, claimed that *the fork'd tongue of the Dragon, consum'd while in its still fresh and animate state, imbues the spoken word with an ineluctable influence over the minds of those who hear it.* More modern texts hazarded that the brain of such a creature might confer cunning of such crystalline clarity as to verge on omniscience. Still others insisted that the right fibrous or lymphoid tissue would grant limitless physical strength, and a small number even suggested that one of the dragon's unique bodily chemicals was the key to controlling forces so primordial that they had yet even to be named.

To Jorg, these rumored potencies mattered less than the reputation they comprised. He nurtured none of the Empire's martial ambitions nor any of the Academy's determination to leash the world. He wanted only to balance the scales of affection so that he and his family might be looked upon as the equals of any other Imperial citizen. With that vision as his guiding star, he struck out on a new path.

First came his lessons in blacksmithing, given freely by a neighboring metalworker. Then Jorg crafted the tools that would lift him up into the caves in which dragons were said to hoard their treasures and their young. Last was his choice of weapon. In all his research, he had found no recorded victories over a dragon through the use of arms. Thus he knew that his opportunity, if one existed at all, must come through some other means. On the night of his departure, he revisited the circular laboratory where his parents' retort sat and he stole as many poisons and paralytics as he could carry.

Rumors and fables were his guides thereafter. He followed them westward, making his way with painstaking slowness through the crumbling and spartan human settlements that marked the cradle out of which the Empire had grown. In those towns that still had the need and the capacity for smithing, he would ply his trade until he had a large enough store of resources to continue. In those that didn't, he did any task that wanted doing and moved on as soon as he could.

After a time, the ground under his feet softened and he saw the tops of trees just over the horizon. Briefly he detoured to the south through the halfling lands to confirm his course. Though they quibbled somewhat over the particular details of what he chased, they assured him that there were great winged serpents that lived in the cliffs facing the western sea. So he made for the edge of the continent. As he traveled, he cast every moment and every decision in tempered iron so that they would be with him always, never realizing that in doing so he was building the bars of his own prison.

***

Officially the Show opens at sunset, but it begins in earnest an hour later under the bigtop. Glyn is the first act, then Zula, then Andra, and then, for the finale, Jorg.

By the time he enters, the tent smells of sweet smoke and bitter beer, of salt and cinnamon wine. Chimes and squeals drift in from the smaller attractions outside, but the inside falls to a giddy hush when the audience hears the thumping footsteps of the stolen drake. Jorg enters first, half-crouched and walking backwards as if even a moment's lapse of attention will release his hold over the beast. Then Cary appears, and all but the brashest or drunkest patrons take a step back.

Even with all of the oddities in the capital, none of them has ever seen anything like Cary. In the torchlight, his scales glimmer like plate armor and his eyes glint with an untamed energy. The traffic think involuntarily of the old legends: of knights crushed to death within their crumpled breastplates, of maimed and bloody maidens, of men turned to blackened skeletons in the blink of an eye. For Cary, it's all a game, and he snorts and shakes his head to tell Jorg that he's ready to play. But what the audience sees is a wild and agitated horror that stands twice as tall as its hardened trainer.

In the space of two heartbeats Cary settles into the center of the tent and paws the ground, and the throng catches its collective breath. Jorg gives the signal, and Cary roars so loudly he can be heard on the palace balconies three miles off.

Jorg signals for fire before the crowd can gather itself. Better to keep them off-balance and have them miss a trick than risk boredom, is Kody's philosophy. So Cary rears his head back and opens his mouth, while Zula, unseen in the wings, summons a geyser of flame so close that it stings Cary's tongue. From then on it's a choreographed dance between the three of them, no less intimate or harrowing than a trapeze act. Jorg signals the tricks and trusts that the others will obey; Cary leaps and snaps in time; and Zula fills the tent with spears and waves and cannonballs of fire. Together, they shoot down balls of cotton that Jorg tosses into the air; they roast a boobrie, from which Jorg takes a charred bite; and, for their finale, they trace a spiraling hoop of fire in the air so that Jorg can leap through it.

After the performance, while Kody and the roustabouts slowly herd the Show's clientele back toward their homes, Jorg leads Cary into the darkness to feed him, calm him, and salve any minor burns that he may have sustained. Tonight, Andra is already waiting for him. He sees her shape in the dark and waits for her to speak first, but she only looks at him briefly before Cary nuzzles her and she turns her attention to the drake. Jorg pulls his flask from his pocket and takes a drink to quell his irritation. He says, "Are you here to help? Or to play? I need to get him bedded down."

"I was thinking about what you'd said," she replies

without turning away from Cary. "About going forward. This place used to be forward for you, didn't it? The Show?"

Jorg nods. "Mm."

"It used to be that for me, too. Even now, I can't go back."

"So now do you understand why I'm still here? Forward or nothing. Some roads lead on, and some reach a cliff. This is as far as I can go."

Andra smiles to herself. "Well, you do have a drake. Maybe you can fly."

"I'd sooner jump off it," Jorg replies. There's so much bitterness in his voice that Andra reaches out to him.

"Jorg, no. You can't mean that," she says.

"No? Why can't I? Can you tell me where I'm supposed to be? Me, a one-handed smith who has a one-ton mouth to feed and no other prospects to feed it than to go out there every night and pretend to be someone I'm not?"

Cary squirms beside Andra. She softens her voice. "Maybe we can change your act, then. If we talk to Kody —"

"Kody doesn't give a gremlin's ass about anybody but Kody. You know that."

As if in accordance with some miserable design, they hear Kody calling. "Andra! Andra, I need you—now!"

"I'm here!" she calls back. Then she says, "Please, Jorg, we can think of something. There must be a way out."

"There is," he says thickly. "In fact, I'm going to get it tonight."

Then Kody is among them, saying, "Andra, good—there's someone I need you to meet. He's young, but he says he wants to join us and help the Show. Come."

"Kody, please. Jorg and I—"

Even in the dark, the change in Kody's expression is unmistakable. "I don't believe that I was talking about Jorg. Now, unless you have some pressing emergency to attend to, I'd like you to come with me."

She acquiesces. After they leave, Jorg goes through the motions of tending to Cary. He never notices the night quieten around him. His thoughts are too loud. But he knows how to silence them.

Once he's confident that his drake is settled, Jorg changes out of his costume and makes for the capital wall. The larger part of the crowd has already returned, but there are still a few troublemakers and invalids amongst whom he slips in: some giggling teenage couples, an isolated and staggering drunk, a cowled crone, a father carrying a sleeping child. He can barely make them out in the dark and they can barely see him, but they serve their purpose well enough. When they reach the wall, the gatekeeper takes one look at them and, in his boredom, marks them all as citizen stragglers and hurries them inside. Thus Jorg enters the city without having to give any account of himself or his purposes.

It takes him the better part of an hour to navigate the silent streets of the lower quarters, make his way through the Imperial district, and arrive at the Academy. Its frontmost towers loom dark and silent against the night sky, but firelight and the sounds of metals and liquids still drift from the windows at the core of its campus. He selects one of the structures from memory and enters it as though he belongs there. Whether due to destiny or the resoluteness in his step, no one challenges him. He climbs to the fourth floor of the tower and proceeds to the room at the end of a dim hall, the lock of which he easily picks. Once inside, he steals a smattering of lethal poisons from the Academy for the second time in his life.

When Jorg leaves the room, he is as bleak and immovable as a mesa. He is also distracted and half-blinded by the ache inside his chest, which is why he doesn't see the old woman in the cowl who has followed him from the Show.

Waiting in the shadows, Andra watches him walk to the end of the corridor and into a stairwell. Then she enters the room that he has just left.

There she finds something like a library. Wooden shelving runs the length of the room in orderly rows, every subdivision of which is labeled with names and dates that Andra can barely make out in the dark and that mean nothing to her. She searches hopelessly through two aisles in the hopes of discovering Jorg's purpose before, in a third, finding that his single-mindedness has facilitated her task.

On the ground in front of her sit four racks of stoppered glass test tubes. She sits to read their labels. All are marked as being some years old. They each also bear a single word that discloses their function: DISORIENTATION, AILMENT, PARALYSIS, DEATH. Of the four groupings, only the latter has any missing phials.

Andra puts her head in her hands, and sorrow for Jorg echoes like a bell inside her. After some moments its peals soften, and she remembers: Harold and Coner, berries and roasts, audiences and fakes. She steadies herself, breathes, and thinks until the river of her thoughts empties into an open sea that is either faith or surrender or self-delusion or all three. Though it's less than she had wanted, she takes the hope that's at her feet and prays that it will be enough.

IV: The Needs of the Show

Over the next weeks, the Show plays several more profitable nights outside the capital before the crowds run thin and Kody decides to move on. In that time and throughout their subsequent travel to the mining and manufacturing towns of the near north, Jorg maintains a constant and pitiless intensity that frightens Andra. She knows that his mind cannot be changed.

Nearly two months after it leaves the capital, Kobold Kody's Frontier Exposition and Tonic Show puts on a one-night performance for the tired-eyed domestics and farm-hands of a town so small that it barely merits a name. As Kody often does in such rustic circumstances, he simplifies the Show for the sake of expediency and profit. The performers go on without makeup, and the fairground is set amid the wagons so that it can more easily be built and unbuilt within a single day.

Some in the Show prefer this looser and more frantic pace. Jorg does not. It sends him off-kilter. He forgets himself and misplaces things. This night, he has misplaced his flask. Again, he suspects Andra. Again, he finds the missing item without confronting her. This time it is in the pocket of his costume pants, and though he doesn't remember putting it there he does remember what he put into it. The poisons from the Academy will serve their purpose. This will be his last performance. He is ready for the end.

Due to their rural surroundings, Kody keeps the big top stored in its wagon and lets his artists play their roles in the open air. Thus Cary faces no obstacles when, after watching Jorg drink and fall as Andra foresaw, he snatches Jorg's motionless body from the ground, lets loose a cry of pure, unchecked agony, and flies into the night.

Having seen all of it once already, Andra has no desire to witness it again. By the time Cary disappears from view, she is already in Jorg's tent sorting through his things by candlelight. Kody finds her there after the crowd has been mollified and sent home. "Thank the sky," he says, holding open one of the tent flaps and sweeping his hat off in relief. "For a minute there I was worried I'd lost you, too."

She looks up from the object she's holding: a small dagger of sorts with a metal loop for a handle. It's a piece of mountaineering equipment known as a piton, and she has seen it before. It is the blade from her first vision. Now there truly is no going back for her: her journey back to Pol has begun. "No," she says to Kody, "you haven't lost me. Yet."

Her last word sticks in Kody's ear like a buzzing fly. His eyes harden as he looks at her and steps fully into Jorg's tent. "Well, now, this is odd. Unless my memory fails me, not long ago you tried to talk me into sending Jorg away. Yet here you are, helping yourself to his estate while his body is still warm. Why don't you tell me what you're thinking, dearest Andra?"

"It's just a memento," Andra says. "Something to remember him by." She holds up the blade in her hand. "I don't want all of it. Just this one piece. That's not too much to ask, is it?"

"No, I suppose not." He frowns to himself, then turns his displeasure back towards her. "But if you see anything like this again—and I mean *anything* like this—you tell me the whole story, down to every last detail."

Andra waits for his seeming altruism to unmask itself

and become the self-regard she knows it is. She is not disappointed.

"I mean, hell, Andra! That was our finale that just flew off!" Kody continues, pointing with the hand that holds his hat. "That was what the people came to see! If you'd told me Jorg would *die*, I could've done something! I could've found another trainer or chained up his animal. At least I could've tried to set it up so that the drake was what killed him." He sees the judgment in her face and rolls his eyes. "Oh, don't be like that—we both know we couldn't have saved him, and a man can only die once. So why waste it? We could've put on an unforgettable drama, but instead we look like fools. Think of what this does to our reputation, Andra. Can you imagine if this had happened back at the capital? It would've ruined us."

He puts his hat back on and sighs. "Well, it's done now. I've had acts run out on me before and I'll be damned if this is the one that breaks me." Then he fixes Andra with his most serious glare and says, "But I need you to tell me what you see. Do you understand? I know that I may not be your favorite person. But right now this isn't about what you need or what I need. It's about what the Show needs. If you see anything like this ever again, you'll tell me, won't you?"

He has nothing more to say. Andra sees as much and knows that she has at least half-succeeded. Kody doesn't know what she's done, doesn't know that Jorg may yet live. But she can't break character. She knows there will be more to come.

In her mind she hopes and prays that Jorg still breathes. Aloud, all she says is, "Oh, Kody. Whatever I see, I'll tell you. I promise."

The Barbarian

I: All That We Cannot See

It takes only a moment for Glyn to assess the sight that greets him when he crests the ridge. Ahead lies an isolated homestead, besieged by a goblin raiding party. At his feet, a half-filled basket of herbs rolls this way and that in the wind, which bears to him the sound of a lone woman's scream. In an instant, his mind's eye plays out the scene: the woman, likely a widow, had knelt where he stood, doing her best to work the unforgiving land of the frontier. By chance she had looked up from her labors and had seen the goblins skittering over the top of the far hills. She had done the only thing that a lone frontierswoman could do: She ran.

Glyn sets a grave frown upon his face and sprints to meet his enemy. His footfalls pound the dry turf but the goblins hear nothing, so fixated are they on their prey. He grabs one of them in his meaty fist, roars with fury, and tosses the goblin bodily against the corner of the woman's small cabin, where it crunches sickeningly and goes still. This, at last, draws the attention of the others. They abandon their assaults on the cabin's door and turn to face their adversary.

Tall he stands, and broad, both features exaggerated in contrast to the hunched and wiry forms of the goblins. Glyn wears only a pair of soft leather boots, a loincloth of the same material, and a sword that remains sheathed on his back. His fists do their work, as he dispatches one snarling creature after another until one of them swings a curved blade that takes the barbarian by surprise. Though his fierce instincts save him and he dodges back at the last moment, the hooked shortsword still traces a thin line of blood across the warrior's brawny chest.

Glyn lets out another roar, not of pain but of warning: He will not accept this insult passively. The armed goblin attacks again, but this time Glyn is ready. He claps the blade flat between his palms and, with a single sharp twist, snaps the goblin's weapon in half. For a moment they all stop, and there is no sound but the beating of Glyn's untamed heart. Then he snarls and tosses the broken blade aside. Within a moment Glyn has the goblin suspended in midair, one of his hands wrapped fully around its neck.

He turns his steely eyes to the rest of the pack. For a moment, they waver. Then, as one, they break and run. He lets the unconscious goblin in his hand fall to the ground. Gently, he knocks on the cabin door. It opens haltingly at first, but when its inhabitant sees her savior she throws the door wide and embraces him.

After an ovation that is for the most part lukewarm and perfunctory, Glyn and Zula, who is costumed in a peasant dress and a blonde wig, duck back through the cabin door, jog into the Show's bustling backstage, and break character.

"Hard crowd," Zula says. She waves a hand in the direction of the stage and the torchlight there dims.

Glyn shrugs. "These people are far from the frontier," he says. "The stories we tell are not their stories."

The goblins arrive next, having waited to clear the

stage until the lights fell and their ringmaster took the spotlight to close the Show for the night.

"Jack!" Glyn calls out. "I'm sorry. I meant you no harm. Are you well?"

One of the goblins stops and smiles. "Ah, Glyn," she says, "you are forgiven." She shudders, and with a sickening crunch her bones knit back into place. "As always, no harm has been done." Jack smiles again and places a thin hand on Glyn's arm.

"The mind may speak with words," Glyn tells her, "but the heart speaks through the hands." He kneels and gently takes Jack's hand in his. "Jack, please tell the others that I wish them well."

"I will, Glyn," Jack says. "As always." She grins again and makes her way to the goblins' traveling warren.

He and Zula pick their way back to the tent that serves as the shared human dressing room. There, Etain finds him and treats his wound with a poultice made from pulverized anole cartilage. "Are you alright?" she asks. "Tom didn't cut you too deeply, did he?"

Glyn smiles down on her. "No, his aim is as careful as ever."

"Enough, you lovebirds," Zula says, her frontierswoman's garb already half-off. Underneath she still wears her pyromancer's costume, a sequined thing that makes her seem to be a flame herself when she performs.

Glyn and Etain blush as they speak their denials in a jumble. Before they can gather themselves enough to offer any clarification or extenuation Andra is there saying, "Glyn, is this a good time? Kody sent me. He wants to see you."

He pulls on a shirt and a pair of pants after shedding his loincloth and prop sword. Together he and Andra leave the chatter of the dressing room behind them. He and

Kody have long understood that each is a last resort of sorts for the other, and so they have, by unspoken agreement, stayed largely clear of one another. Kody's summons is therefore a source of some anxiety to Glyn, and he makes no effort to hide his discomfort as he and Andra enter Kody's tent.

Their employer is still flushed from delivering the close of the night's performance, and they can see sweat standing out against his powdery stage makeup. "Well, don't just stand there, you two, come in," he says, and he waves them in with one hand while he shrugs off his costume frock coat with the other. They enter and sit on a pair of softwood chairs. Kody sits on his cot.

"Now, Glyn," Kody begins, "I want to start by thanking you for being with us for so long. I know that we didn't exactly find each other in the best of circumstances, and I know it would've been fair of you to leave me at any time. You've been a big part of the Show and a big part of my success. I thank you for it."

Glyn has never heard a speech like this before, but he understands its meaning clearly enough: Kody is disposing of him. "I don't understand," he says. "Why are you saying this?"

"Glyn, Andra here tells me that you'll be leaving us soon." Kody looks Glyn in the eye as he speaks, and there is no pity or sympathy in his gaze. "We'll be hard-pressed to go on without you, especially now that Jorg is gone and you're our finale. But Andra tells me that you'll be bringing back something that'll more than make up for your absence."

Glyn looks from Andra to Kody and back. Kody remains brisk and businesslike. Andra looks sorry enough for both of them, and this saddens Glyn even further. Though he does not believe in future sight, he does believe in omens and signs, and in the ability of humans to read those signs.

Outside the tent he hears the sounds of the Show folding back in on itself in preparation for travel, and he says, "I don't want to leave. Where would I go? My people are gone. Our very footpaths have been retaken by the land, and the land itself has been taken by your Empire."

"I know—this is never easy. But there's no rush," Kody replies. "I want you to know that you can take all the time you need." He reaches in his pocket and holds out a handful of coins. "Just in case I don't get to see you again, I hope that you'll take this as a sign of my appreciation."

But Glyn has no love of money, least of all money that is meant to compensate for a hurt that was committed knowingly. He stands, turns his back on Andra and Kody, and walks out, into the night and into his thoughts.

★★★

Glyn is nearly unique in the world. Few of his people survived the Empire's expansion, and fewer still were born in time to be raised in the old ways, as Glyn was. As he puts the camp behind him, he experiences something that only a few others ever have: the concurrent sensations of being completely sure of where he is and yet recognizing almost nothing around him.

For untold centuries Glyn's people lived primarily through the use of two magics. One of these, a sea magic, served them in the summers. For the rest of the year they roamed the east, south, and west in small familial bands. In these smaller groups they relied on a second power, bestowed by the eye of the turul. They fed one of the bird's eyes to every child who was of age, thus making that child a man or woman and conferring on them the turul's dual role of hunter and protector. To enable them to fulfill these responsibilities, the sacred eye of the migratory turul gave Glyn's people an infallible compass: the power to see the right path even when there were no landmarks, when the light faded, or when obstacles blocked their way.

When Glyn ate his eye it was slick and hard and cold, and he nearly vomited. He swallowed against it, swallowed again, and willed his body to accept it. It was a fierce will, one born of a clear and proud desire to wear the mantle of adulthood. Glyn would tell the stories of his people rather than simply hearing them. He would arrange the rites instead of simply performing them. He would ensure that those who came after him would be able to see the land as he saw it: as a free and open world whose shimmering skyborne rivers of light and color led always towards home.

Now his people are near to extinction and he has nothing to preserve or defend, nothing to restore or renew. Yet as he sits beside a meadow stream in the dark and thinks on his conversation with Kody, the signs of home are visible everywhere around him. Once, his people believed that these signs were as permanent as the order of the seasons and that, like the seasons, they would always serve true. His people were only half-right: the signs themselves have survived, but nothing else has. Now Glyn's turul sight, like the labels of the fraudulent elixirs and bogus tonics that Kody sells to dazzled carnival goers, suggests the imminent presence of comforts that either are entirely unreal or else provide too little relief and carry too bitter an aftertaste.

He sits with these thoughts until they leave him, borne perhaps by the silent water or diffused into the cool air. After some time, Andra finds him and sits beside him in the tall grass. Together they watch the moon's reflection sway in the stream.

"I know this stream," he tells her eventually. "It's less than a day's walk from our meeting place."

Andra knows he can't mean the Show. She turns to him and asks, "Our...?"

"The Sceal Cosa'in. My people," Glyn replies. "We met at the north coast every year when the weather warmed. Each arriving group was no more than thirty, but together we were thousands."

As he explains, his back straightens and he seems somehow to gather the whole world into his telling: looking to the north to suggest the sea, picking out tufts of grass to serve as families, sweeping a hand across the meadow to signify his people in their multitude. In all of their years together Andra has only known him as a reserved man. Seeing now what it is that he has been reserving, she is surprised by awe and affection. She moves as little as possible so as not to disrupt him.

"Our time here was different," Glyn continues. "It was the only season when we would trade with your people, your Empire. It was the only time when we met our cousins and learned of their travels. The days were full of laughter and the nights were full of song, and the sea sustained us completely. We ate dried wrasse gills for their magics, and together we drank teas made from saltwater and ate the animals who swam there.

"Some nights we lay on the soft sand and traced the stars until sunrise. Some days the elders told tales that lasted until sunset and could only be spoken above the sound of waves. We found rest there, and healing."

Though he stops before he can say how this story ends, Andra knows already: *And now, none of them can ever truly go back, not even the few who are still alive.*

She waits for the sounds of crickets and frogs to drown out this mournful thought. Then she says, "I didn't mean to hurt you earlier, Glyn. I didn't want to tell Kody what I'd seen, and I didn't want him to tell you. But I had to."

She hopes that Glyn will finally look her in the eye, but instead he stands and looks back to the north. "If he abandons me at last," he says, "then let it be here. I will go to the shore and live there until my days are over and my people come to take me to the next world."

He turns to leave her, but before he gets far she calls to him. "I can't stop it, Glyn. Once I see it, no one can. But there is one thing that Kody didn't tell you: You won't be alone."

Even in the dark, Andra can see the soft double burden of hope and unbelief settle onto his shoulders. She stands and says again, "You won't be alone. I promise."

And then, together, they make their way back to the camp.

★★★

Once, before Pol, Andra met another of Glyn's people. The woman was wrinkled and dark of skin and hair and eye. She stayed in Andra's town for several days, conversing with the townsfolk and trading trinkets with them; the rest of her people camped near the horizon. She only spoke with Andra once. Their conversation did not go at all as Andra would have predicted.

It was not that she expected the so-called barbarian to request a reading. As unschooled as Andra may have been in the ways of the broader world, even she knew better than that. Still, when the woman entered her parlor and sat down across the small table on which rested the trinkets of Andra's trade, Andra did not expect her to smile as though she were the one hiding a secret and say, "Tell me, O seer, do you know how this world came to be?"

Something about the situation turned Andra cagey and hesitant. She didn't know whether to play along or to ask the woman to leave. And if she did play along, she didn't know how to proceed. As she normally would have? As though their roles were reversed? As one practitioner observing and learning from another?

In the end, Andra fell into an indeterminate place between all of those possibilities. Without knowing her own motivations, she told the woman the creation story that she'd learned as a girl. "The world was once shapeless and empty," she said, "until the great god Sol, to show his strength and glorify himself before the lesser gods, brought forth light and land and life. Every day for six days he invented new miracles and was pleased by what he had done. And when at last he was satisfied, he rested."

"That's right," the old woman replied, "he rested. But he was the only one, for although the light was beautiful and strong, it never ceased. And so the animals never rested, the plants withered, and the soil baked. Had the process of creation ended there, one-sided, the whole world would be as harsh and spare as this town of yours.

"So we are fortunate," the woman continued in a voice that was both sad and sweet, "that the lesser gods and goddesses looked down as well. When they saw what Sol had done, they saw a world crying out in anguish. The skies burned, the rocks ached, and all life cried out for respite."

This addendum was new to Andra, whose elders had always concluded with Sol's triumph. Suspicion and interest competed in her as the old woman continued. "Seeing this, the remaining gods and goddesses draped the skies in a soft, downy blanket, easing the light and bringing shade and relief. When these, the first clouds, finally burst, the rain purified the land and revitalized its weary inhabitants. But then the clouds were gone and the daylit frenzy resumed."

Andra did not need this woman to tell her about the significance of clouds and rain. Dust, dirt, clay, rock—these were her constant companions. As a child, each storm had registered as a unique event in her history. Even as an adult, the most water she had ever seen in one place aside from those rare and enthralling downpours was in the bottom of the town well.

Once the sun passed above the mountains in the morning, it hung over Andra and her people like a high, drawn-out note in a terror song. Their food consisted of small game and the few gardened edibles that they could defend from the native weeds and the dry air. Their possessions amounted to a collection of makeshifts and approximations. Andra had never entertained the notion that ease and comfort might be native to the world. She could never have afforded to.

All in all, the old woman's story struck Andra as an idler's daydream. Yet she couldn't bring herself to spurn the lure of an alternative world of mildness, peace, and balance. So, as the effortful sounds of metal striking stone and dirt continued outside, Andra listened intently to the end of the woman's tale.

"Seeing what had become of their fine clouds, the other gods convened and decided that a more reliable form of aid was required. First they lavished water upon the land in seas, rivers, lakes, and streams. These would give themselves to the sky from time to time so that new clouds could form, but they would also remain on the land for any who needed them.

"After the gods and goddesses laid the waters down, they shaded their eyes, reached out as one, and tugged gently at the sun until they pulled it back down to its home beneath the earth. When the light had finally gone, all the world exhaled. The hunters, unable to see in the dark, laid down their fevered bodies and slept. Then the smaller creatures shed the fear of pursuit and huddled together to dream. Even the leaves softened against the mild air. After some hours, the sun returned, and the world rose to activity again. The lesser deities watched and waited. When the proper time came, they returned the world to tranquility a second time. Again and again they repeated the cycle, until the sun learned to set whenever Sol's creatures had exhausted their strength and to rise only when they'd recovered it. Only then was the work of creation truly finished.

"And *that*, young one, is how the world was made: both life and rest, both action and repose, both the land and the water, both the glory of day and the kindness of night."

As she fell silent, the woman reached towards the center of the table and placed an object of such surpassing beauty as Andra had never seen before. It was glossy and hard-surfaced, a spire barely the size of a fingertip and thinner than a thumbnail. It curled open at one end; the other spun to a point. Its outside was striped like pale rock and yet, somehow, the inside glowed like sunset. It was a tiny seashell, exquisite enough to fill Andra with both awe and anemoia.

"What is it?" she asked.

"A sign," the woman answered, "of all that we cannot see—and of all that we choose not to."

II: Blood On The Sand

The following day, the Show arrives at the hollowed-out port that marks the Empire's northernmost expansion. There, on the coarse gray sand by the gray sea, it tinkers itself together and comes to life. Zula opens the main act with a rousing pyromantic display and is met with half-hearted applause. Kody, supplementing the diminished cast, follows her with feats of marksmanship with knives and arrows. The crowd is hardly moved at all. Andra's dour prophecies inspire some to leave. Glyn's performance in the finale is booed outright.

Though unpleasant, this is far from the Show's first inhospitable reception, and few of the cast carry it with them to their beds. Instead, they all think of Jorg, one way or another. They have been nearly a month without him.

For some, Jorg's loss weighs heavily. With the possible exception of Lady Ugok, with whom no one can communicate, the entirety of the sideshow is sorely shaken by what happened to him. Their jobs seem simple and safe enough, but Jorg is a reminder that the Show will always be a mercurial home.

Others have moved on more rapidly. Kody, for one, seems almost not to remember that there ever was a man named Jorg. For very different reasons, Andra, too, has grown cagey about the subject of the Show's dragon-tamer. Even now she maintains an anxious silence whenever his name is spoken. And then there is Glyn, who always believed that Jorg lacked the balance required for a long life. Though he would not have guessed the details of Jorg's passing, the fact of it did not surprise Glyn.

So when Glyn wakes to a clear morning after the Show's inauspicious coastal debut, he does so without a single thought of Jorg to trouble him. Well-rested, he walks along the beach towards the town, which is a mile or more to the east. When the Show arrived the day before, the town was screened by a mist that gave it the aspect of a cut-paper lightbox, and Glyn wants to see it in the light of day.

He is still several hundred yards away when he hears shouting from behind a dune and, unthinking, rushes to its peak. It takes only a moment for him to assess the sight that meets him there. Ahead, three pale, dark-haired men in workers' clothes stand in attitudes of anger, surrounding someone who has fallen to the sands. At his feet he sees tracks leading from Kody's camp, and in between the men's curses he hears a woman's cry for help. He recognizes it as Etain's voice, and he sprints to save his friend.

But the men on the beach are not his goblin costars, and they turn to Glyn immediately. "Keep back, barbarian," one of them warns. Though the man is smaller and thinner than Glyn, he is also coiled more tightly than his companions, and there is malice in him.

Glyn comes to a stop two arm's lengths away from the men, who move to form a wall between him and Etain. In the distance Glyn can see the outskirts of the town: a few small boats on the sand, some smaller homes, and a seemingly disused pier with a sprawling hut at its far end. Other than the three men and Etain, he sees no activity.

"My friend," he says, "I carry no ill will for you. If we have offended you, we ask your forgiveness."

The first man takes a step forward and says, "To hell with you and your apologies! To hell with the Empire and its clowns! We built this place for you and you left us to rot. Now you come back and mock us to our faces and call us 'friend'? We know what type of friends you Imperials are!"

From behind him, Etain cries, "Please, I told you that we aren't part of the Empire. I told them, Glyn, I did!"

The leader snaps his head around to her. "Then why do you travel under its icons?" Then, to Glyn, "Why do you spread its lies and call it entertainment?"

Glyn has asked himself the same question many times. He has no answers to give. His complicity weighs heavily on him, and he shrinks into himself and holds out his empty hands in a gesture of surrender. "Just let us go in peace," he pleads.

But the leader of the three men has no such intentions. He advances on Glyn and the other two follow, emboldened by their hatred and Glyn's show of passivity. Glyn's heart skitters in his chest. Despite his role in the Show, all he knows of true combat is its awful residue: a legacy of broken bodies and bloodied soil. His only hope as he watches the three men surround him is that his strength will discourage them. But then their leader draws a knife and Glyn's hopes burst into panic.

The man on his left swings a fist at him and Glyn's feet slide in the sand as he tries to step away. Still, it's only a glancing blow that catches him, and he grabs the man's arm and flings him to the ground. Then he sees the knife in the corner of his eye and twists every muscle to escape. But without the benefit of choreography and rehearsal, Glyn is helpless. The blade passes easily through his loose tunic and opens an arc of blood from his sternum to his right hip. Etain is screaming, and Glyn is down on the sand, struggling to rise on his left hand and knee. There is nothing in his mind but the gentle whisper of the ocean and the sadness of death.

Yet before the curtain can fall on Glyn's life, a woman's voice stops the men where they stand. "Boys, you get away from that man—and I mean *now!*"

With that, the attack is over. The leader, bloodied knife in hand, turns towards the newcomer as if reluctant to be seen. Likewise there is reluctance rather than strength in his voice when he says, "This is none of your concern, Nickelette."

Glyn sees that the woman has ignored this protest. As she advances through the edge of the surf, she spreads her long fingers and the air seems to hum. "I said leave him," she repeats, "and I meant it."

Though none of the men admit their surrender, they circle away from her and Glyn, keeping well inland. As Nickelette reaches Glyn, his assailants give one last empty threat and flee. Nickelette breathes out and the humming fades, leaving only Glyn's panting and Etain's shaken sobs.

Up close, Glyn sees that his savior looks nothing at all like a warrior. She has a boy's haircut and sharp, round eyes behind copper-framed glasses. She is also nearly as tall as he is, and she offers herself as a crutch for his injured right side as he stands.

"Thank you," Glyn gasps. "Our camp is—"

"I know where your camp is," Nickelette says. "We ain't going all the way back there." She nods her head towards the ramshackle building on the nearby pier. "That's me there, and unless you're a fool you'll want to get patched up sooner rather than later."

"Thank you," he says again, and he lifts his left arm for Etain, who has rushed to support him as well.

"Are you alright?" Etain asks. "Oh, Glyn—I'm sorry. This is my fault, I should never have wandered off."

"He ain't alright yet," Nickelette responds, "but he will be. And quit your crying. Walking on the beach wasn't a crime the last I checked. Not even here."

Together they shuffle through the sand and walk with heavy, thumping footsteps down the pier to Nickelette's makeshift house. As Nickelette shifts Glyn's weight to allow her to open the door, Etain wipes her eyes and says, "I don't know how to repay you."

"Well, that's alright. You don't owe me nothing, so there ain't no need," Nickelette replies.

"But Miss Nickelette—"

"Nic. My friends call me Nic. Now let's get this big old boy inside and see if we can get him sewn up." She looks back and grins. "I just hope my other patient don't mind a little company."

III: The Other Patient

Out at the far edge of the pier, Nickelette's house is an unruly conglomeration of driftwood, broken and cast-off pieces of ships, salvaged doors, and various sundry reclamations. The sound of the sea surrounds it. Glyn breathes in the smell of salt and wood, and his head clears somewhat. Now that he is safe, his side hurts with theatrical intensity. He allows Nickelette to lead him towards a small room in the back of her home, where an unshaven and emaciated man is seated at a square wood table by a window that looks onto the water.

"Who—" Glyn struggles to ask, only to be cut off as the man turns toward him, gives a start, and croaks, "Glyn, Etain—what are you doing here?"

When Etain sees the man's mutilated right hand, she calls his name and rushes over to him. "Jorg! You're alive! But you're so thin. We should tell Kody. Or, wait—is Cary with you?"

"You all know each other, huh?" Nickelette asks as she gestures back and forth between them with a roll of gauze. "I probably should've guessed—not a lot of reasons for a man to have a full-grown drake as a pet."

"Yes," Jorg says in a rasp, "we know each other. And yes, Cary's here. He goes out fishing during the day, brings us back some dinner at night. Stay long enough and you'll see him."

Etain claps her hands together in relief. "That's wonderful! We've all missed you so much. It feels like so much has changed. The crowds don't seem to like us as much anymore,

Ugok had to draw a whole new pile of advertisements, and the camp seems so empty at night without you and Cary. Kody moved Glyn to the finale, but I'm sure he wouldn't mind switching back to his old spot, would you, Glyn?"

Jorg stands, sending his chair clattering to the floor. "No! I won't go back!"

They all pause and watch him, Etain still clasping her hands together, Glyn seated on a small bed with his arm raised, Nickelette partway through tending his wound.

"Sorry," Jorg says. He averts his eyes and busies himself with the furniture. "I'm sorry, I didn't mean to shout. But I can't—" He pauses to cough. "Don't tell anyone I'm here—not even Andra, and especially not Kody. Let them all think that Jorg the dragon-tamer is dead." Everything set back in its place, he sits and turns again towards the window and says, "After all, he is. And that's for the best."

Nickelette works on Glyn's bindings in a silence that lasts until Etain plucks up her courage and kneels by Jorg's side so that she can address him at his level. "What happened to you, Jorg?" she asks.

He tries to face her but can't quite manage it. "I'd rather not talk about it," he says with tears in his eyes.

Having finished Glyn's bindings, Nickelette jerks a thumb towards the door. "I think we should be getting you two back. Think you're up for it?" Glyn nods, and Etain tells Jorg that she'll be back. But Jorg keeps his eyes pointed towards the sea until he hears the sound of Nickelette's front door closing.

"Good old Jorg has been doing some metalworking for me ever since he recovered," Nickelette explains on their walk back to the camp. She taps her glasses to demonstrate. "I'd hate to lose him. But who knows—I sure didn't plan on him showing up, and it looks like you all didn't plan on him leaving."

Etain holds up a hand to block the sun as they walk. "I didn't know…" she begins, but then trails off.

"Didn't know what?" Nickelette asks. "That he was unhappy?"

"We knew," Glyn says.

Both women look at him. Etain looks away first. "We're all unhappy," she explains, clutching the dark tile around her neck as though protecting it from some harshness. "At least, I think we are. The Show isn't really a happy place, most of the time. We—" She pauses. "For most of us, this is the best we can do."

Nickelette hums thoughtfully. "I guess I never gave it all that much thought. Every circus I've ever seen looks like it's happy enough, but I suppose an outsider would never really know."

Those are the last words they speak until they arrive at the campsite, where the goblins stop their handiwork to spread the news of Etain and Glyn's return and Glyn's injury.

Before they part, Etain hugs Nickelette and says, "Thank you so much, Nic—you saved us. If there's anything we can do for you, we'd be happy to help."

"I'll certainly give it some thought," Nickelette replies as she stands back. "I'd ask for a free ticket to the Show just to see you perform, but, well, you've just about put me off it. So I guess it's so long for now, Miss Etain.

"And as for you," she says to Glyn with a wink, "you keep yourself out of trouble, sea-drinker."

Up until that moment, Glyn had felt little but shame and sorrow around the woman who calls herself Nic. His vulnerability in her presence reminded him of all that he has been robbed of: the chance to train in the arts of men, the material signifiers of adulthood and prowess, and his place in an ancient line that would have furiously defended one of its own. These thoughts have left him more keenly isolated than he has been since his childhood. They have made him feel pity for himself.

But Nickelette's last comment to him is a message. She knows something about him and his people. If he wants to find out what that thing is, he knows, he has to see her again.

IV: The Ashes of the World

After another ill-received performance, Glyn gathers wood and builds a fire under the clouded skies. He sits by himself for some time thinking about Nickelette until his castmates begin to join him. Etain and Andra arrive first, followed by a cluster of goblins, some of whom carry their children in slings on their backs. The women and the goblins talk around the fire, their conversation drifting softly in and out like the tide. Glyn listens more to its hush and its undertow than to the words.

Coner approaches the group during a lull in the conversation but remains at the edge of the light cast by the fire, where his scales and slitted eyes are visible only in flickers. "I'll never understand it," he says. "Why buy a ticket for a show you know you'll hate? All those people tonight—I don't think I saw one of them smile. The next time I meet someone sensible, it'll be the first time.

"And you," he adds, speaking to Glyn, "why go to all the trouble of building a fire out here when Zula can give you one for free?"

All eyes turn to Glyn, but instead of rising to the challenge, he turns to Andra. "What do you hear?"

In her surprise it takes her a moment to respond. "I'm sorry—I don't quite know what you mean."

"The world is always speaking. If you listen to it now, what do you hear?"

Coner shifts his weight from one foot to another, and all of those gathered hear the slide of his shoes over the dirt.

"Crickets," Andra says. "The waves. The fire."

And, indeed, the fire crackles and sighs in the stillness. The sound is elemental and comforting. Glyn nods and says, "This is a living fire—and also a dying fire. It speaks." He gestures to the embers floating into the sky and addresses the whole group. "It breathes. Zula's fires are ghosts, neither living nor dead. They cost nothing, it is true. But that which is destroyed matters just as much as that which is created. The ashes of the world should not be forgotten."

Coner shifts again, grunts to himself, and leans towards the fire as though to sit and join them. Instead, he thinks better of it and bids them good night.

They sit unspeaking for some minutes. Then Jack the goblin says, "Will you tell us a story, Glyn?"

"Yes," he says after a moment's thought, "I will." His chest rises and his eyes fill with clarity, just as they did the night before when he told Andra about his people. "What story would fit this night?" he asks.

"Tell us about the blue-capped ifrit and the sleeping maiden," Jack says.

"Tell us about the goldhorn and its flowers," another goblin suggests.

"We're very nearly to the coast," Etain says. "Do you know any stories about the sea?"

Glyn nods and says, "My people had many stories about the sea. But the sea is far older than stories. The sea and the sky both are older than the world. They were not created, and so they cannot be destroyed, not even by the gods.

"In our travels I've heard many tales of how the world was born, but none of them tell it fully. It is true that the jealous spirit Sol created sun, soil, and life for his own aggrandizement; and that the other spirits opposed him for the sake of the animals of the land and the sky. But that is not the end of the story."

Glyn looks at each member of his audience in turn. With each, he watches the play of the firelight on their face until he can see them as a unique individual rather than a variation on a pattern established by their species, sex, age, or role. Jack's skin is dry, perhaps from the fire, but her silver-blue eyes are youthful and they're so bright that they almost luminesce in the dark. Her child is angular and its ears are still outsized for its head. It blinks slowly, as though deeply content. Etain has a soft, light-colored halo of vellus on her cheeks. In Glyn's opinion it forms a charming contrast with the rest of her hair, which is almost as thick and black as his. Andra's face is soft, so soft, and it hides so much.

Around he goes, and as he looks he continues his story. "Just as we all have a voice of our own," he says, "and just as this fire has a voice, so, too, do the spirits have voices. Sol used his to speak the day world into being, but the other spirits used theirs to bring balance to what he had made. When he saw what they had done, he vowed in his vanity and fury that they would regret speaking against him. So he gathered his powers and snatched up the voices of all the other spirits, and he scattered them in the numberless empty shells that were abandoned by the creatures of the sea. That way, the other spirits could never frustrate him again.

"Sol's fit of rage exhausted him for an eon. But he has been recovering his powers ever since, and there will come a time when he has fully restored himself. With no other spirits to oppose him, he will bring about our destiny, the fated time: the end of nights. This is why my people have always sought balance. It is why we listen to the shells that whisper in our ears even though they appear to be empty:

Each one contains a breath of a spirit who opposed Sol and brought balance to the world. With luck we will find the breath that teaches us their wisdom before it is too late."

His story told, Glyn leans back and allows his audience to return to themselves. Within minutes most are lulled by the warmth of the fire and the cool of the night. The goblins leave first, followed by Etain, so that Glyn and Andra are the only ones who stay while the fire burns itself down.

"Is that true? About seashells speaking with the voices of the gods?" Andra asks. She has waited for the sake of this one question and for what its answer may portend for her.

In place of an answer, Glyn rises and kicks sand over the fire. "I saw Jorg today. He told me not to tell you. Why did he say that?" he asks.

"You've seen him? He's alive?" She steps close enough to look into Glyn's face. "Oh, Glyn," she says, "tell him I'm sorry. Tell him it was the only way. He'll understand. And tell him—tell him that I don't despise him. Will you do that?"

"I will. But I don't want to live with him," Glyn says. "I would rather be alone."

Andra reaches out to him. "I'm sorry, Glyn. He's not the one I meant when I said you wouldn't be alone. I didn't know he would be there. I'd hoped he was still alive, but I didn't know. And that he would be here of all places! But please, give him a chance. He's not what he seems. Trust me."

"None of us are what we seem," Glyn reminds her. "Kody seemed like a good man. To your people, I seem like a barbarian. To me, you seemed innocent. Jorg doesn't trust you. What did you do to him?"

Andra lowers her hand. She looks away, toward the smothered fire. "You said that we shouldn't forget the ashes of the world. I'm one of those ashes. Years and years ago, someone burned my world down around my ears, and ever since I've been blown about on the wind." She turns back to Glyn. "But now I have a chance to act for myself again. An ending is coming for me, just as it did for Jorg. I want to turn it into a beginning. That's why I interfered with him. And it's why I need to know if your story tonight is true.

"The gods who counterbalanced Sol's actions—are their powers real? Are their voices trapped in seashells? I know you may not believe me, but I saved Jorg. That's what I did to him. I just want to save myself as well."

Glyn turns away toward the dark. "When I return," he says, "I will tell you."

Andra watches him walk into the night and thinks of her coming confrontation with Pol. The threat of it has been a cage on both her life and her hopes. Now she knows that such cages can be negated, that one can become an escape artist and walk through their bars as though walking through thin air. Already she has performed such a trick with Jorg. Now, after hearing Glyn's tale of the other gods and their sunken voices, she sees a way to do the same for herself. She returns to her tent filled with thoughts of seaborne whispers and deep magics. When she goes to sleep, she does so with her seashell held tightly in her hand.

V: The Story-Keeper

Glyn finds Nickelette near her house, standing up to her chest in an ocean that glows blue as a noon sky. She looks so at home that he briefly wonders whether she might be some sea creature herself, a rogue selkie or nereid. Then the bloom on the water fades and she is just a woman in the dark, sloshing towards him through the gentle tide.

"Hello again, sea-drinker," she calls to him.

"We call ourselves the Sceal Cosa'in," Glyn calls back. "Story-keepers. Not sea-drinkers. Not barbarians."

In another few steps, she is before him, dripping and grinning and waiting for him to ask the questions that have been swimming in his mind for the whole of the past day.

He gives in. "Who are you? Why did those men fear you? What do you know about my people?"

"Not as much as I'd like to," Nickelette replies. "Come on inside. I'll show you around."

Glyn sees Cary's sleeping form underneath the pier as they walk along the tideline.

When they approach Nickelette's home, she puts her fingers to her lips and says, "Talk quiet—your friend sleeps pretty light."

She opens the door and takes a strange metal object from a hook on the wall. It has a handle that separates into two thin stalks, between which runs a curl of metal wire. Glyn hears the same humming noise that he heard when Nickelette rescued him, and the wire at the end of the device begins to glow.

"This is why those men ran," Nickelette murmurs, holding up the light. "It's like lightning, only not as strong. I got it from a river fish way down in the southwest that the dwarves know about. Here, I'll show you its bones."

She leads him into a large room filled with papers and books and a slew of odd-shaped contrivances whose purposes Glyn can't even guess at. In the honey light of the glowing filament she leads him to a skeleton that has been mounted on the wall. Longer than Glyn is tall, the skeleton is an undulating parade of ribs that terminates in a vicious skull.

"This is what I'm here for—what we were all here for, back before the Empire decided it didn't want us," Nickelette quietly explains. "We were supposed to take ships out onto the open ocean and find new magics that we could bring back to the mainland, water magics. They sent us out here with soldiers, workers. Hell, they paid our way. But I guess they must've been in a hurry, because a few of our ships sank and a few more came back empty and then all our help from the capital dried right up. That just about soured most of us on the Empire, and on the ocean, too.

"The way I see it, though," she continues, moving the light so that it's between them, "nothing's really changed. Those people in the capital were never on our side in the first place. They never even tried to get to know this place. They just wanted us to find them some new power they could use to feed their ambitions. But that water out there has secrets just waiting for me—I know it does." She holds the light higher and smiles. "I'm the proof."

"Those secrets are not yours to take," Glyn whispers, angry and disappointed. "If we live *with* the water, *with* the land, then they will live with us. If we take everything precious away from its home, we will all find ourselves without a home as well."

"Then teach me," Nickelette whispers back fiercely. "I've met your people, I've seen how they live. You all've got something better than magic. You've got knowledge. Teach me."

Glyn shakes his head and brushes past Nickelette, though she hisses at him to wait. He makes his way to the door. He wants to get outside and clear his thoughts, but a mist is rising off the water and Glyn can find no solid sight upon which to anchor his mind.

Nickelette, light still in hand, finds him easily and tells him again to wait. "I can help you," she says. "I don't know when your people are coming back—they don't exactly keep to a regular schedule these days—but they know me. Look, I know you got a raw deal. I only got a little taste of what happened to you all, and I'm still stinging. But I swear I don't bite. At least stay the night and think it over—I don't want you getting turned around in this fog."

But Glyn's turul sight is unobscured, and it has already oriented him toward the camp. "I thank you for your aid," he says, "and your hospitality. Live in balance." He steps into the mist and is gone.

★★★

The next day starts with misting rain. Kody declares that he's taken the hint. He wants the Show packed up and on the road. Glyn and the goblins do most of the heavy work, as usual, but there's enough to keep everyone busy. All of the performers are responsible for their own costumes and props, from Andra's fake silks and imitation crystal ball to the warm-weather plants that Coner uses in his exhibit to make himself seem exotic rather than piteous. In addition, there are the thousand small implements that maintain and undergird the Show's physical reality: the plates and utensils, the bedding, the provisions, the hand tools, the spare fittings and components, the stage makeup and signage, the candles and torches.

The rain persists through midmorning, by which time sweat coats Glyn and tiny pearl raindrops shine pale on his hair and clothes. He is glad for the work. It quiets the keening that the events of the preceding days have washed into his chest. His instinct tells him that too much is out of kilter, foremost his presence at the coast during the wrong season and without his people. The whole area feels largely unreal to him, a dramatization of itself, perhaps, or a trick of the light.

Bound up with this thought is Nickelette. Glyn wants to believe that some of his people are still together and that he could reunite with them one day. Yet he mistrusts Nickelette and fears that she would merely use him in the way that all of the Empire's people use the world around them.

These thoughts harry Glyn, but in time they are hushed and then muted altogether by the steady, repeated act of wrapping his hands around barrels, trunks, and boxes and lifting them into place. The gray weather and manual labor likewise turn all of his colleagues into silent silhouettes of themselves. Glyn pays little attention when he notices one such silhouette standing out beyond the Show's front gate. Yet something about its bearing eventually snags him. He approaches, and as he does he sees that the silhouette belongs to Jorg, who is mostly hidden under a thick, ink-dyed cloak that keeps him dry in the lingering rain.

Glyn greets him and says, "Have you come to retake your place in the Show after all? Kody will be very happy."

"No," Jorg replies, and then again, "No. I won't leave.

Nic is helping me to become whole again. On the inside, I mean," he clarifies, nodding to his right hand.

"Good," Glyn says, and he means it. "I was saddened to watch you fall that day, but I was more saddened to watch you stand against yourself every day before."

Jorg nods as if to affirm some insight in Glyn's words. "Yes, I guess you would've been. I should've sought you out—any of you, really, but especially you, Glyn. You know what it's like to lose. But it's not too late, is it? We still have time, you and I. We can still help each other."

"Gain and loss visit every life," Glyn says, matching his words to the slow in-and-out roll of the waves. "And I will not join Nickelette, not even if you are the one who asks me to. You may trust her. I do not."

"She said you'd probably say that." Jorg reaches inside his cloak and produces a worn waterskin. "She said to give you this. Try it."

The skin is warm in Glyn's hands. He uncaps it and takes a small sniff to ensure that it isn't more of Jorg's liquor. What he smells is salt and iron, fermentation and freshness, a watery dark green and a light latent sweetness. Tears of recognition prick at his eyes. It is the ocean tea he remembers from his childhood. He drinks it down eagerly.

The rain is gone. The sounds of the Show's disassembly, already softened by distance and mist, vanish completely. In Glyn's mind, he can only see summer; in his heart, he only feels love. There is no magic in this beyond nostalgia, but the nostalgia is powerful enough that it subsumes him completely into memory.

He remembers his young brothers, sisters, and cousins taking their turul eyes the night before they all left the coast for the last time. He remembers eating his own turul eye, remembers the antic lightshow that unveiled itself before him as though revealed by a rising curtain. He remembers his family leaving in the morning. He remembers them heading sharply southwest for the first time in their lives in order to avoid the capital and its growing dislike for the Sceal Cosa'in. He remembers saying goodbye.

He remembers traveling into unfamiliar lands with richer soil and darker trees, remembers seeing chimney smoke rising from impossibly small halfling villages along the horizon, remembers the smell of autumn. Then, he remembers the rest.

With no warning, Imperial soldiers broke up his family's camp one morning near the dwarf lands of the far southwest. They took the men and ordered the rest to transport themselves to the badlands in the southeast, the ogre lands, the dry rock. Glyn's father spoke back to them and was clubbed across the face and led away bleeding. Glyn, newly a man in the eyes of his people, was still a boy to the Empire, and so he marched with the women and children and an armed Imperial escort to the re-location camp on the other side of the continent.

That year it seemed that there were settlers every-where. Glyn's amputated family was further pierced by the harsh treatment they received along the trail to the east. True to their name, it was customary for the Sceal Cosa'in to pass their travels by telling the old stories amid the comforting sounds of craft and weather and fire. Glyn remembers that there were no stories that year. There was only the confused wailing of the children, the grim whis-pers of the women, the pulse and ring of his own stoical silence as he prayed that his family would be reunified.

It was not to be. The Empire was no illusionist, who, having cut Glyn's people in half, would make them whole again through some ersatz sorcery. The body of the Sceal

Cosa'in had been sundered and it would not find healing. Several of his family died before they reached the relocation camp. Several more died after they arrived. The Imperial soldiers who oversaw them gave them little food and water and allowed them even less freedom of movement or activity. When one of Glyn's people fell ill, the soldiers forbade the women from leaving to find medicinal herbs, and the illness spread. When one of them died, it was common for sadness to take another shortly thereafter. The women did all they could to buoy the group's faltering health and morale. The soldiers did more to stamp it down.

After a month or so, Glyn's mother took him aside and told him to leave. "You are a man now," she told him through cracked lips, "one of the few the Empire did not take. Because they are gone, you must do what they cannot. Go. Use your new sight and find any god or mortal who will come to our aid."

So Glyn waited for the cover of night and then ran. If the soldiers noticed that there was one fewer captive the following morning they cared too little to give chase. Glyn traveled for weeks alone under the harsh southeastern sun. Knowing little else in the way of succor or safe harbor, he made for the northern coast. In doing so, he led himself directly back into Imperial territory. Once there, he followed the skyborne signposts that his turul sight afforded him. Through luck or providence, these markers led him one twilight to a midcontinent hilltop from which he saw, spread below him, an early incarnation of Kobold Kody's Frontier Exposition and Tonic Show.

The Show was much smaller then. Even so, it clattered and trembled with such manic activity that from afar Glyn mistook it for a spirit gathering or some other type of unearthly convocation. Its flickering lights looked like

fireflies or will-o'-the-wisps. The sounds of carnival bar-
kers and startled women rang in his ears like jackals'
laughter. In all his people's deep store of myth, there was
nothing like it. Even so, one glance told him the only
thing he needed to know. This thing, whatever it was, did
not belong to the Empire.

In the settling darkness, Glyn crept nearer through
the weeds and tall grass and watched the Show draw in
one customer after the next. Like the ocean lapping at
shoreline rocks, the milling crowd rippled around the
Show's meager exhibits: Etain, skittish and young,
twisting in the half-light; a hunchbacked juggler; an old
gnome swaying and playing a hurdy-gurdy; Andra taking
calloused palms in her hand in the hopes she would read
anything good therein; a blindfolded basilisk chained to a
stake; and, everywhere, Kody.

Kody performed blade tricks using small knives that
he produced from the same peacoat he would still wear
years later. He walked through the crowds advertising and
selling the Show's eponymous tonics and elixirs. He
played up the other acts. He welcomed newcomers and
farewelled those who were leaving, and he wheedled tips
from as many of them as he could. When at last the Show
released its customers into the night and exhaled, it was
Kody who took a torch and left the carnival ground and
walked straight up the hillside to Glyn's hiding place.

"Hello there, young friend," Kody said to him as he
approached, stopping at a respectful distance. "You've
been quite patient, waiting on this hill all night. You
should know that I don't typically look kindly on free-
loaders such as yourself. My personal view is that anyone
who enjoys the Show ought to buy a ticket. But somehow
I sense that you're a special case." He saw the startled look
on Glyn's face and tapped his temple. "Catsight. Helps

when you're a military scout. But don't you worry—that's all in the past. I'm just a showman now."

Glyn shifted his footing in case he needed to run.

"Whoa—no need for that. I know your people," Kody told him. "You all were always kind to me, even back when I was scouting for the Empire. You know we didn't always call you barbarians, don't you? We used to get along just fine. For a while there, I thought we always would. But then—well, seeing how much we took from you, I figure I owe you as much as I can give."

"We need help," Glyn blurted out. "Soldiers found us. They took half of us and sent the other half to the orc lands. Many of us died on the journey, and many more have died there. My mother sent me to bring back help."

Kody took a step forward and parted the weeds with one hand to bring the light closer to Glyn's face. "My apologies, little friend. I know all about what's happened to you, but the Show doesn't have room for everyone, and I'm in no position to lead a raid. Is your mother with you? I could take the two of you, at least. Two would be al-right."

Glyn shook his head.

"Well," Kody sighed, "then I guess it'll have to just be you." He held out his hand. "Come on. My name's Kody. I don't quite know what I'll do with you, but I'll find some-thing."

But Glyn shook his head again, stood, backed away. "My mother sent me to find help," he repeated firmly.

Kody stood as well. "Aw, kid, don't be like that. Trust me, this is the best offer you'll find. The Empire did wrong by you and yours. *We* did wrong. And believe me, there's worse coming. But the Empire is the only—and I mean *the only*—game in town. I can't start up another one all on my own, but I can help you play the one we've got. Let that be enough."

Glyn could barely even conceive of what Kody was asking him to do, let alone could he do it. He had lived his entire life in the presence of those who loved him. To voluntarily trade that for a lonely existence as a living curio in some traveling pageant of grotesqueries would have been an act of outright insanity. So, with Kody calling to him and telling him that it was already too late, Glyn turned his back to the Show and ran.

It had taken him weeks to travel from the camp in the southeast to the nameless town where he'd seen the Show. His return took only half as long, driven as he was by fear and the fresh knowledge of how little he could hope to accomplish on his own. When he arrived, he learned that Kody was right: It was too late.

Glyn was no stranger to death. He had seen it in the stupefied faces of the drowned and the old. He had seen it in the curled self-pitying bodies of those whom violence or sickness had cut down. But he had never seen a massacre.

He did not count the bodies whose blood stained the tan stone carmine red, nor did he attempt to identify them or deduce the cause of their deaths. The Imperial guards may have been among them, or not. His mother may have been among them, or not. The corpses may have represented the sum total of his people, or not. All he knew was the vulgar buzz of the swarming flies, the ticking of the deathwatch beetles, and the unbroken disregard of the open, endless sky.

There were no burial rites he had the power to perform in that rock-crowned desolation and no one with whom to perform them. There were no stories to tell that could make sense of what he had come upon and no audience that could appreciate them. Nevertheless, he stayed there for three days and nights, insensate in a paroxysm of grief. On the fourth day, Kody picked him up bodily from the ground and carried him back to the Show's meager caravan, which he had left several days to the north.

For weeks, Glyn recovered in the dubious comfort of one of Kody's rattletrap wagons. At nights, when the Show rested or performed, he gave careful thought to everything that had happened and settled on the conclusion that the sun god Sol had reawoken, as his people always feared he would. Without the sea-bound gods to keep the balance of the world, there would be no telling what manner of sorrow or depravity would arise. The apparently total extinction of his people was just one example of the former; Kody and his squalid Show were an example of the latter.

Glyn came to believe that, in this new world, he himself was the aberration, the lone survivor of the old world and the sole inheritor of the old ways. For that reason he could not bring himself to leave Kody's protection. He felt that the world was tilting, becoming skew-floored, and he feared that this new cant would kill him as easily as it had his kinfolk. More than his dedication to the keeping of stories, more even than his refusal to waste the life that his mother had saved unknowingly when she sent him off to find help, Glyn was simply afraid to die. Kody may have aided the Empire that broke Glyn's nation and he may still have traveled under the insignia of that same Empire, but he had offered Glyn a safe haven, and Glyn decided to take it.

***

Slowly, the wave of memories recedes, and Glyn is returned to himself and the graylit beach and the slow, soft rain. He has no doubt that Nickelette's tea is authentic. No imitation could have affected him so strongly. He caps the skin and looks down at it in wonderment. *There is only one way for her to know how to make this*, he thinks. *She truly has befriended my people. They are, after all this, still alive.*

Jorg, who has been watching Glyn closely, reads his hesitation as indecision and hands him a jagged white tooth as long as Glyn's thumb. "Nic also said to give you this as a memento, if you wouldn't come back. I think she took it off that awful sea monster she has hanging on her wall."

Glyn smooths the beads of rainwater from his hair. In his heart, he feels stronger and less afraid than he has in years. "I will go with you," he tells Jorg. He turns the tooth over in his fingers. "But there is one thing I have to do first."

He finds Andra sitting inside one of the painted wooden wagons, waiting either for the rain to pass or for the Show to be on its way. She greets him warmly, then asks, "Do you have something for me?"

"I do," he says, and he leans towards her to hand her the tooth.

Inside the wagon it is surprisingly quiet, the rainfall being too gentle to echo on the roof or walls. When his hand touches hers, he says, "You were right. I won't be alone here. I don't know how this will help you or Kody, but I hope it is enough to repay you."

Andra smiles thinly, and there is a quaver in her voice when she says, "It's not for Kody. It's for me. I only told him that you'd bring back something of value. I didn't say who it would be valuable for." She takes the tooth from Glyn and moves her closed hand to her lap. "Thank you for bringing me this, Glyn. We'll miss you, but I'm glad that you've found something better."

"I haven't found anything yet," he corrects her, withdrawing from the wagon. "Only the hope that something can be found."

"Well," Andra says, and squeezes the tooth in her palm, "even hope is better found than lost."

Glyn nods, steps back, and takes one last look at the Show. In the dim light and the rain it looks almost innocent.

He turns, and Andra is the only one who sees him go.

VI: Just a Name

Nickelette is standing under the eaves of her roof and watching the rain dimple the water when Jorg and Glyn return. Off in the distance, Glyn sees Cary's silver wings flash through the rain like soundless lightning. Nickelette smiles when she sees them and says, "Well, color me relieved. For a while there I thought I'd scared you off. I know I can come on pretty strong sometimes, and I want you to know I don't blame you for being cautious."

Glyn hands her the waterskin. "You've met my people," Glyn says. "They taught you how to brew the ocean leaves. Can you drink it?"

"Nope," Nickelette replies without losing any of her cheer. "They trust me with some things, but they've still got their secrets. I figure either they'll tell me one day or else they won't. Meanwhile, we learn from each other and help each other out. I give them any news that comes my way and they help me sell my research to other people who believe like I do."

"What is it that you believe?" Glyn asks.

At this, Jorg turns to look at Nickelette. Since his foiled suicide attempt, he has kept to himself out of both exhaustion and a fear of jeopardizing the generosity of his hostess. But now that Glyn has asked the question, he feels that he needs to know the answer.

Nickelette doesn't speak right away. Instead, she takes off her glasses, cleans them on her shirt, and puts them back on. "I suppose you could call me an agitator," she says. "Or even a heretic, maybe. I used to think the Empire had room in it for things that were different—or even strange or mysterious. I guess that sounds foolish to you, Glyn, but it's what I thought. But those people truly think that they know every single thing. They don't have any room at all for anyone who won't fall in line. And, well, I've never much been one for falling in line.

"So I guess what I believe is, if we're not good enough for them, we'll just have to be good enough for ourselves. Or, well, I will. You've got your own people all set up and waiting for you," she says to Glyn, "even if they don't know it yet. So, listen, just stay. You don't have to tell me anything. I won't try to force you. I'm just a little jealous, is all. You know so much that I want to learn, but you're right: just because I want something don't give me the right to try to take it."

Her speech sets Glyn's heart at ease. Although he agrees to wait on the coast for his people to return, he also says, "I cannot live in your home. I will make my own shelter."

Nickelette looks out at the cool rain and the wet sand, then she looks back towards the town proper as if to see whether Glyn's attackers are advancing for another try. She says, "Are you sure? We're coming up on winter and all. You may not like it out there on your own."

"Thank you. I will make my own way," Glyn says stiffly.

"Glyn, stop," Jorg says. "Don't hold yourself apart like that. So what if we're not really your people? Right now we're the only people you've got. Are we really so bad?"

Glyn looks away and blushes. He explains, "Among my people, an offer to share a dwelling is also an offer to share...other things."

Nickelette laughs delightedly at the misunderstanding

and claps Glyn on the shoulder. "Don't you even worry
about that, my friend," she says. "You may be handsome
and tall, but you're not exactly my type, if you grasp my
meaning—and if not, I'll just say that my meaning is the
only part of me you'd better grasp. Now come on in and
let's see about finding you someplace to sleep."

★★★

When Kody discovers that his barbarian is indeed gone, he
goes to find Andra, eager to learn what replacement Glyn
has left in his place. He finds her standing up to her mid-
calf in the chill water and gazing at the gray horizon. "You
know," she says without turning, "part of me almost
thinks I could live here."

"What, a delicate desert flower like yourself?" Kody
replies from the sand. "You'd be drowned right out."

The joke falls into a nervy silence. Neither of them is
confident of what is about to happen, and so both of them
wait for the other to make the first move. But after a few
moments Kody's impatience to leave for the next town
gets the better of him and he says, "So that's it for Glyn,
huh?"

"It is."

Kody licks his upper lip. "What'd he leave us with?"

"Just a name," Andra says over the sound of the surf.
She wants to turn and face Kody, to look him in the eye,
and to deliver the lie to him directly, as he has to her so
many times. Yet she is so fearful of what she plans to say
that it is all she can do to stand without shaking. Never
before has she tried to deceive Kody or purposefully taken
any action to speed the arrival of the destiny she foresaw
for herself. The thought of doing both at once squeezes
her throat and flattens her lungs.

She now has two of the items from her first vision: the blade, which belonged not to a dragon slayer but to a man who would have been one; and the shard of lightning, which was not petrified but fossilized. More vitally still, she has the knowledge that Jorg is alive, and she has Glyn's story of gods and seashells. Together all of this has given her a granule of hope, and that hope is enough to weigh her down against the panic that sweeps through her in gusts.

So again she says, "Just a name," and then she takes one more breath to steady herself.

"Pol."

The Fortuneteller

I: Only Catastrophe

Little changed in the immediate aftermath of Pol's visit to Andra's nameless desert village. Every evening the sun descended leisurely beneath the western horizon as if it might finally be satisfied with what it witnessed during the day and might therefore grant some blessed reprieve to the gaunt dirt farmers and broken-down bricoleurs who were Andra's people. Every morning it reappeared from behind the mountains in the east with the startling suddenness of a card sharp producing an ace from within a sleeve. Andra concocted a plausible story about Pol's purposes, persuaded her neighbors to believe it, and tried as best she could to forget the entire fiasco. Before long, the incident passed from gossip into local memory and life returned to its familiar rhythms.

Only Andra's dreams were different. Every night she saw with perfect clarity some minor setback or major tragedy. Though most of these featured subjects who were strangers, she also sometimes saw her own neighbors. The first several of these visions Andra dismissed as mere nightmares. But when she dreamt of failed crops, the crops would soon fail; and when she dreamt of strife, it would soon follow. She knew then that her dreams were not dreams at all but foretellings, and that she had become in truth what she had long pretended to be.

When her neighbors came to Andra's curtained parlor to have their fortunes read, they found her new predictions to be different in their blunt and artless precision from the mystical counsel that Andra had given before. The change kindled in them a wary distrust. Andra had once seemed to be continuous with her surroundings and with the people who inhabited them. But her new visions cast an overbearing fatalism upon her and set her apart. Andra's neighbors were united in their dislike of her new persona, and this dislike doubled upon itself when her predictions came to pass.

"You've gone too far now," an old friend named Elen told her once while they were drawing water from the well. The two of them had grown together as children, Andra pale and dark-haired and quick with words while Elen was ruddy and blond, a child of the sun who was already bound to a life as a fieldhand. "Trying to scare sense into us was one thing," he said, "but you can't fulfill your own prophecies and expect us not to notice."

Andra paused for a moment with the well rope in hand and the bucket suspended partway to the light. "Is that really what you think of me?" she asked.

"What else should we think?" Elen replied.

Before she answered, Andra finished hauling up the bucket and dumped the water out into clay pitchers that the two had brought. "Believe what I say," she said at last.

"How can I, Andra? No part of you makes sense anymore. First an aristocrat from the capital comes here just for you. Then you change the way you talk to us. And now this? I want to be your friend—I *am* your friend—but I don't understand," Elen said, and Andra understood from his earnestness that they were opposites in more than appearance alone.

In her role as a fortuneteller, she had mapped subtle

and shifting mazes of human intention and passion. She had accustomed herself to thinking about what lay around the next corner and what larger design might be at work. But Elen worked the land and believed in what he could hold: the clothes on his back, the spade in his hand, the meal at the end of his day. None of Andra's explanations could satisfy him. They would only be words and thus less substantial even than the air. If she could not reach him, she knew that the rest of her people were lost to her completely.

Like Elen, none of them could fully explain why she had changed. Instead they traded conjectures among themselves like shrewd customers bartering with a higler. Some said that her time with Pol had led her to believe that she was above her station. Others claimed she had always been that way. A few even declared that she was simply in need of a husband.

All such speculations were soon resolved by events that began when a detachment of soldiers arrived to rest in the town. They would stay only one night, they said, after which they would resume their pursuit of some band of marauders that had been scouted nearby. Andra had neither encountered nor witnessed any such hostile elements. In the past, some few travelers had even claimed that there was no threat in either the itinerant goblins or the leather-skinned orcs or any other non-Imperial nation nearby. Nevertheless, Andra's people were loyal to their rulers, and most of them held that the presence of the soldiery and the concomitant inflow of capital rendered such questions incongruous at best and suspect at worst. Thus, the detachment arrived to an enthusiastic welcome.

Andra did not share in this enthusiasm, distracted and unnerved as she was by the vision she had had the night before. It had featured a band of Imperial soldiers who embarked out from her town in pursuit of some group of fugitives or scofflaws. She saw them as clearly as if they were spotlighted before her on some grand theatrical stage: their sunburnt and stubbled faces, their whitened hydraskin armor, their adventuresome martial camaraderie. In her vision, they tracked a small party of natives into the wind-lashed north, marching for hours on end and pausing only to cut for sign or otherwise reorient themselves towards their prey.

Andra saw the sun go down on them and the light cool to blue. She watched them chew hardtack and dried meat and handfuls of seeds, taking their water from those seeds as did the dipodomys. When they had eaten their fill she saw them bed down on soft pale soil under a wash of stars. She saw the night wheel above them and begin to brighten with the arrival of day. Then she saw the cool ground silently open up and deliver all but a few of them into the waiting maw of a beast that so horrified Andra that she woke.

So when those selfsame soldiers crowded into her parlor that very day, with their same shining armor and their same swagger, Andra's mind went blank with confusion and an overpowering sense of wrongness and danger.

"Greetings, soothsayer," the captain said. He was a man who looked as if he was accustomed to taking what he wanted from the world. He tossed a handful of coins on the table and grinned a hard grin at Andra as he continued. "My men and I have little time here and we're seeking leisure. Will you entertain us?"

Some of the assorted soldiers laughed and jostled one another, but Andra's vision from the night before was a screaming urgency in her mind. She would not play the docile maiden. "You mustn't follow them," she said. "Whoever you're chasing, whatever the reason—don't go."

For a moment there was the sound of metal on leather as the men shifted, unsure of how to respond. Then their captain spoke again. "This is a poor notion of entertainment," he said. "Our mission is our sacred duty. It comes down to us from the Emperor himself, may the light shine on him always. To abandon it would be to abandon our own honor. But I am a generous man, and I choose to believe that you did not intend to insult us thus." His grin returned, and this time it had a serration in it. "Try again, seer. Give us a proper fortune."

Andra in that moment was like a woman tumbling down a mountainside after a misstep, knowing that she was moving down the wrong path and yet wholly unable to arrest her terrible momentum. "You can't go," she said. "Please, you have to believe me—it isn't safe. I understand about honor, I do. But there is no honor awaiting you if you go. There is only catastrophe."

She wished dearly that she could have simply given the men the anodyne half-truths they had come for, as she would indeed have done if she had not already witnessed their deaths. They would have believed those half-truths and would have been satisfied by them. But the weird alchemy of human expectation works both ways: Just as it would have lent unearned credibility to her false words and cheap props, it acted on the honest dread in her words and, in the ears of her audience, transmuted her meaning from a plea to something more like a warning or a threat.

"Only catastrophe, you say," the captain said slowly. "And why would that be?"

"I have the gift of future sight," Andra answered in a shaking voice. "I've seen your mission, I know—"

"What do you know?" the captain said in a rush. With a crash, he swept the table clear. "What do you know?" he said again. "Are you an ally of the barbarians? Are there enemies of the Empire in this town? Do not feign powers you don't have, girl. If any true oracles existed, the Empire would know it, just as we know that there are seditious activities taking place near this town."

Andra's breath came like short soft cries for help, like the mewling of some small wounded animal. "But I saw —" she began.

"You saw nothing!" the captain shouted. "You have no powers beyond those of deception! Do you truly think that we're so ignorant, girl? How foolish would we be to believe that you were born into poverty and dust and chose to stay here even after obtaining a power that eludes the Emperor himself? How foolish would we be to not know the face of our own enemy?" He struck her table with his closed fist. "Who moves against us? Who?"

"It was some monster," Andra said weakly. "It lived below the earth and it—it..."

But she could not describe the horror she had seen, not even to herself, and as she trailed off the captain bared his teeth at her. "You've made your choice," he said. "Pray to the golden sun above that you do not live to regret it."

With that they were gone, their appetite for amusement spoiled. In their absence, Andra did indeed pray. As evening fell, she restored her parlor piece by piece and prayed that she had been mistaken. In the dark, she prayed for their safe return. And against her own fears and the uncaring chalk light of the dawn, she prayed for herself. By the time she was done, the soldiers had departed again. The die had been cast.

The following day was blurred by worry and exhaustion. Her neighbors treated her with renewed mistrust. They averted their eyes from her on the beaten path that served as the town's lone road, and none of them came to visit with her or have their fortunes read. She fetched water for herself alone. She washed her clothes alone and hung them to dry alone. She cooked her meals and ate them alone. And that night, when again she could not sleep, she left alone to find the soldiers and save both them and herself.

She walked north for hours under a slow-turning scrim of stars. Near dawn she finally folded into sleep; at noon she woke and began walking again. Soon there was no town on the horizon behind her and no sign of human settlement around her. Sometimes, she thought she saw the marks of the soldiers' passage in the hard ground, but she was no tracker and trusted more to fate than to her own inadequate skills.

In this way she wandered in some approximately northern direction for two days. She survived on dried fruits she brought with her and on such edible plant life as she could find. Never once did she come within ten miles of the soldiers. Only the mountains to her right changed: slowly unreeling past her as she walked, gaining and losing dimension as the sun cast them in various combinations of light and shade. When her food ran low, she turned around, put those same mountains to her left, and struck out for home, consoled by having at least done everything in her power to prove her virtue.

On her return, her neighbors were even more hostile to her than they had been before. Rather than showing her their backs, they glared at her openly and followed her, as though she were some wild beast who might at any moment need to be corralled or cut down. Near her house, one of them, a woman older than Andra's parents and possibly older than the town itself, approached her. "You fooled us all for too long," the woman told Andra. "But they'll catch you. Your days under the sun are numbered, girlie. The Empire does not save its kindness for traitors."

That night, she learned from Elen that the soldiers had returned during her absence. Only two had survived. The captain had escaped the creature in relative good health. His lieutenant was less fortunate. The monster had butchered him, taking both of his legs below the knee and leaving furrows in his torso and thighs that exposed red-gray muscle and white bone. The captain had treated the wounded man as best he could using the town's paltry supplies. He then commandeered a cart and mule, with which he hoped to transport the younger soldier to some surer rescue. Together the two of them left, before Andra's return but not before spreading word among the townspeople of her actions and branding her an anti-Imperial element.

Some of Andra's neighbors were afraid of helping one accused of treason and being marked as traitors themselves. Most heard the soldiers' accusation, weighed Andra's recent change of character and the fact that she had absented herself precisely when the soldiers returned; and decided that she truly had plotted against the Empire. Worst of all was Elen himself, who wore such a look of embittered betrayal that Andra felt she would rather vanish into the mountains and scrape her meals from the rocks than stay and risk Imperial capture and be a daily witness to Elen's disillusionment in her.

So it was that Kody's appearance the next day was near to a miracle for Andra, albeit one necessitated by such circumstances as could never have been sanctioned by a just or benevolent god. She saw Kody in the morning, riding in from the western horizon through the heat, and even before she could make out his features she knew he was somehow larger than life.

He dismounted at the edge of the town and walked his horse down its one dirt road. Unlike Pol, he greeted all those whom he saw and even paused to exchange words with those who had an interest in conversation, some of whom seemed to point him to Andra herself with the angle of their body or the tilt of their head. She sat on a desiccated wood chair under the canvas awning that sagged outside her home and watched him. In those days, his face still had some of its youth and his dark hair had not yet started to gray. Still, she saw plainly that he was no innocent. There was something coiled in him, something whiplike, some snake's tongue that was constantly testing the air in advance of a bite.

By and by he reached her. He took off his hat with one hand and held out the other. "Hello, young lady," he said. "My name is Kody—what may I call you?"

There was polish in his voice, but Andra knew it for an artifice. She did not take his hand. "What makes you believe that you have reason to call me?" she replied.

"Well, if it happens that your name is Andra, then I believe you'd be the one I'm here for. It seems that you and I have some, ah, common acquaintances."

Andra's breath scraped against her throat. She waited for the trap to spring.

Instead, Kody kept talking. "See, I'm what you might call a businessman, only I happen to be in want of a business just at present."

He paused in a way that seemed to invite a reply, so Andra looked him up and down with his dusty clothes and his lone horse, and she said, "And how can I help? I have little to sell and I have no training in any normal trade or skill."

"Ah," Kody said, and he held up one finger, "but it's no normal skill that I'm after. Just yesterday I happened to share a camp with some soldiers who told me a very interesting story. The main character of this story was a woman who pretended to be clairvoyant in order to hide her involvement with enemies of the Empire. They said that this woman threatened their safety and that she or one of her accomplices made good on the threat.

"So I rode here to see this hotbed of subversion for myself, see if there might be some rogue who would enjoy a change of scenery. But now that I'm here, I'm starting to think that maybe those soldiers were wrong about you." He paused to wipe the sweat from his forehead with the back of his wrist, hat in hand, and then he gestured about them. "So tell me: is this really some run-down insurgency run by a scrawny girl and comprised of people who barely have the time to draw their bread from the earth? Or do you have the gift?"

Andra smiled with a bitter sadness. "What I have is hardly a gift. And it won't be of any help to you, because you won't believe a word I say. No one does anymore." She stood up and brushed the dust from the bottom of her skirts. "I'm sorry that you've come so far for nothing, but you might as well be on your way. I've already made the mistake of my life. I'd rather not become the mistake of yours, too."

But when she turned to go inside Kody caught her arm, and she saw that the sly mirth was gone from him. He said, "I do believe you."

"What? Why?" Andra asked, distraught and confused.

"Because," Kody said in a voice that was finally just its own raw self, "nobody would ever say something so pitiful unless it was true."

Andra sat back down in her chair and put her face in her hands and wept. Kody simply held his hat and waited for her to speak again. At last, she pulled her hair back from her face and said, "But what do you want from me? I can't tell you where to find gold or jewels. I can barely tend my own garden."

"Well," Kody said, and he smiled, "you can just leave all that to me. All I need to know is whether you'd rather stay here than leave with me. If you'll come along, we can be on our way by tonight. If not, I'll hold no hard feelings. But you can trust me when I tell you that you have something that people will pay good money to see, whether they believe it or not. With my help, I'll make sure you get that money—and that the Empire never lays its hands on you."

Andra's head felt light. *If ever this curse could be of use to me*, she thought, *now's the time*. She stared at Kody and tried to divine what his influence might portend for her future, but nothing came to her. Knowing no better, she said, "Come inside. Let's at least talk."

II: Everything That Begins

Whenever Andra reflected on the conversation in which Kody persuaded her to leave her home, she knew that the game had been lost the moment she invited him to talk. Kody may have proven himself as a scout, called himself a businessman, and established himself as a showman, but Andra discovered over their long years together that he was in actual fact a salesman. At first, she wondered whether his voice was imbued with some uncommon magic that originated in a siren or bergsra. But in time she came to believe differently. The longer she observed him, the more she saw that there was no part of Kody's charm that did not trace back to the man himself.

Together they traveled the continent collecting performers, castoffs, free spirits, oddities, and anyone else who could be pressed or gulled into joining Kody's nascent Show. They found Jorg and Coner sharing a bottle in a beggar's hovel that stood out like a scabrous blemish amid a field of pastel wildflowers. Kody tracked them down by following Cary, the drake. When he entered their shack, they were slumped against a wall, filthy and morose. "Hello, gentlemen," he said to them while Andra stood in the doorless entryway. "By any chance would one of you be the owner of that fine ashen drake outside?"

Jorg thunked the bottle onto the dirt floor. "And what if I am?" he asked in a sullen, deadened voice.

"Then I," Kody said with his same smile, "have a job opportunity that I'd like to discuss with you. My name is

Kobold Kody. My associate and I are forming up a traveling theater troupe of sorts. I'd like you to join—you and your friend."

Jorg stood carefully and swayed in place for a moment. Having achieved stability, he stepped to within a handsbreadth of Kody. "So go find yourself some actors," he said. "Or nannies. Fables and fantasies are for children."

"So they are indeed," Kody immediately replied, "but I have no intention of catering to simpletons and sissies." In a glance he took in Coner's scales and Jorg's mangled hand. He said, "Our acts will have adventure and wonder in them, it's true. But they'll also have ugliness and pain, because ugliness and pain are inescapable truths of the world.

"I don't mean to mollify my audiences," he continued. "I mean to overpower them with what I've seen and what I know. And I mean to live comfortably while I do so. Now, I speak only for myself. You gentlemen are free to join me or not, as you see fit. Among the greatest gifts that the shining god above granted us is the power to be as much or as little as we choose to be. What will you choose?"

In the ensuing silence, Andra moved out from the stink of the two drunks and walked to the top of a mild rise, where she sat and breathed in the sweet air while a burning radiance of phoenixes flew overhead. Before long, the men exited the hut and Jorg collected his drake and they were all five on their way.

Next, they plucked Etain from a northern mining town. The weather turned chill there, and the sighing trees brushed Andra almost lovingly with their dark and falling leaves. Etain was just a child then, and she was glad to leave behind the orphans' home where she lived and the hard-walled tunnels where she worked to earn her bed. When Andra first saw her, Etain's eyes were hollow and her hair was blacked by coal dust, and Andra knelt down to hold her until Etain held her in return.

During their travels, Andra saw things she could never have imagined had she stayed in her hometown. She walked through farmlands where the crops reached to her collarbone and stretched to the horizon in all directions. She rose early one morning while in the southwest and, sitting in a wagon, watched a family of elk breakfast on the grass as a mist settled over the land like a coverlet. As she and Kody traveled the continent, the Show expanded from a few loose strays into an entire motley pack. The goblins met them on the road and took up with them instantly, as though by unspoken mutual decree. Glyn arrived in Kody's arms. Harold came on after attending a harvest-festival performance in the soft hills of his homeland. Lady Ugok simply appeared one morning, bereft of any obvious provenance and lacking the ability to give any account of her arrival. And so it went, one year after the next, Kody's Show growing in both size and magnificence, just as he intended.

***

Yet everything that begins must end. Andra knows it. More: she has seen it. One day Kody will have only her and Pol, the three of them dealt together like cards shuffled and downturned on some grifter's table from which only one will be picked out by fate's hand.

With this destiny in mind, Andra stands in the water at the north edge of the known world and speaks the poet's name. This done, she turns and wades ashore and tells Kody of everything else that she's seen: a death among the goblins, the Human Pincushion's defection not only from the Show but from the very ground on which they stand, and Etain's tearful departure.

He listens and nods and understands nothing. Many times he has told her that good illusionists never reveal their secrets. Now she takes his lesson to heart. She does not describe for him her first vision. She does not explain the meaning of the piton; she does not show him the tooth. Kody must believe that her only motive is to serve him and his Show. Until it's over, she will keep her own counsel.

Kody has always treated the Show as his own and done with it what he pleased. But soon enough Andra will see her remaining castmates on their way; soon enough she will find the ancient scale and the box of fire. Then will come the final act, and that act will be hers alone.

The Sideshow

I: The Stage Crew

After speaking with his soothsayer, Kody makes one last sweep of the grounds to ensure that nothing has been mishandled or forgotten. The rain has tapered off but the clouds remain. Kody can't say how long the respite will last. Rapidly, he checks that the horses are fed and watered, ensures that all of his potions have been packed safely, and takes a headcount of all those still in his employ so as to confirm that they are present and accounted for. They are not.

"Where are the goblins?" he asks of no one in particular. Coner and Etain turn to look his way. No one answers. "Where are my goblins?" he asks again, louder. Again no one answers.

He turns to look down the coast in one direction and then the other. They aren't there. He climbs up the beach and the firmer soil upon which the wagons are waiting and looks in and under each of them in turn. He notices several places where the wagons will have to be repainted, but he doesn't find the goblins. Sweat slides down Kody's neck and he sets his jaw against his agitation. Then he hears them.

Off to the southeast somewhere nearby, the goblins are singing. Kody doesn't recognize the song, nor can he understand it. He has never learned the goblin language. Yet he does not need it to know that he is hearing a requiem.

Kody walks toward the sound; his cast follows behind. Within moments they find the goblins gathered in a shallow rut. There are twenty or thirty of them singing and swaying in a circle around Jane, one of their number. All of the goblins but Jane are crouching or kneeling and are holding one another. Many hands touch Jane, but he is held by the earth alone, and he is both silent and unmoving.

Andra brushes past Kody and joins the circle of mourners. Etain follows a moment after, then the Human Pincushion, then the rest, until only Kody and Zula remain at the top of the grassy declivity, looking down. Zula looks once at the massed mourners and once at Kody. She scoffs quietly and makes her way back to the campsite.

Kody takes his hat off as a show of respect and waits for the dirge to end, but his mind is unmoved. As the song continues he shifts his weight from foot to foot. The moment the singing fades, he addresses the goblins. "Is he...?"

"Yes," Jack answers, turning to Kody with sad eyes. "Jane has gone to the other place."

"Hell," Kody says. "Just—hell. I'm awfully sorry. Listen, you take your time here with him. We can get going in the afternoon." He puts his hat back on and turns to leave, but Jack speaks again.

"We must stay."

Kody turns back. Now all of the goblins as well as their human and halfling friends have turned towards him. "Well," he says carefully, "I certainly don't want to rush you, but we'll have an awfully hard time eating if the Show doesn't perform. I think we can all agree that we won't be performing here again any time soon. So I really don't believe we can stay."

"You may leave whenever you wish," Jack replies. "We do not wish to detain you. But we must stay. We will stay."

"Okay. That's okay. Just how long of a stay are we talking about? Can't take more than a day or two to take care of the, uh, rites."

"We stay until the next of us arrives," a dark-skinned goblin child answers from among the group.

"It is our way," Jack adds.

"I'm sorry," Kody says, "I don't quite think I follow. Who are you all waiting for, exactly? And how will they know where to find you?"

"We will wait for the next child," says the goblin named Tom. "The child will know to find us because Jane will meet them in the other place and send them here."

Kody can hardly believe his ears. "You mean to say that you'll all just stay here until one of you has a kid?"

Several of the goblins nod their heads.

Kody looks back towards the horses and the wagons. In his head, he quickly calculates the amount of labor that the goblins do for the Show. Then he tallies the Show's reserves and looks back at the assembled mourners. "Well, much as I hate to say it, I don't think we can wait quite that long."

Now Jack stands, and despite her short stature she seems to tower over the rest of the mourners and over the body of the dead goblin Jane. When she speaks, Kody feels almost as though they are eye-to-eye. "You may leave," she says again, "but we will stay. Jane has gone to the other place, and we must stay here until he sends a new one back to us. It is our way."

Kody takes off his hat once more so that he has something to squeeze. "I understand," he tells the small crowd below him. "I really do. Believe me when I say I'm awfully sorry to see our partnership end like this. I'm just—well, I just wish it could've been some other way."

He takes a few steps back towards the camp, then

stops. "Andra, Coner, Etain, the, uh—all the rest of you, I want to get on the move today if we can, but just come back when you feel the time is right."

Kody puts on his hat and waits, but none of them makes any reply. He stands uncomfortably for a moment, then he nods to them and makes his way to the wagon train. Behind him, another elegy begins.

II: The Human Pincushion

Though the Show leaves the northern coast behind for brighter and more welcoming environs, a pall remains. Without the goblins, the going is much harder, and spirits are low among many of Kody's workers. This is especially true among those who, like the Pincushion, prefer not to be faced with challenging questions or unexpected turns of events.

Kody feels their unrest in his bones like the first sifting dust that presages a landslide. As the Show rides through the slowly rising hills of the northwest, he mulls it over from the driver's box of the stagecoach that leads his wagon train. Before he can reach any definite conclusions, the Pincushion interrupts him.

"Ah, pardon me Mister Kody," the Pincushion says, "I don't mean to intrude or—well, at any rate, I just wanted to know, is everything alright?"

Kody draws a tolerant breath and looks down at the man. The Pincushion manages to walk with a scurry in his step even though the wagons are traveling no faster than walking pace. As he scuttles along he fidgets with a six-inch needle, rolling it between his fingers, testing its tip with the pad of his thumb, sliding it painlessly under the first layer of his skin.

"My friend, things are better than alright," Kody says. "Why do you ask?"

"It's just..." the Pincushion begins. He withdraws the needle from his skin and steps nearer to Kody's seat and lowers his voice. "We've lost two of our biggest draws, haven't we? And now the, you know, the goblins? Aren't you at all worried?"

"Come up here," Kody says and pats the seat beside him, less out of any honest bonhomie than out of a need to induce the Pincushion to sit and thus cease his constant nervous wriggling. The Pincushion sticks his needle through one earlobe and clambers aboard.

"Am I worried? Of course not! These things happen," Kody says, only to pause for an eyeblink when he discovers that he, too, has forgotten the Pincushion's name. "Yes, indeed," he continues, "in business these things happen, my friend. But the old saying holds true: The Show must go on. You just leave everything to your old pal Kody and we'll be just fine."

"Ah, well, yes," the Pincushion says, "but it's—I don't mean to be rude, sir, but I feel slightly as though I may have made a mistake in joining." As he talks, he looks around him as though the wagon is riding through a pack of sleeping bears or as though he fears that a fall to the ground, a mere four feet below, might prove fatal. "It's just, when we met, you said—"

"I remember what I said," Kody cuts in before the Pincushion can finish. He places a paternal arm around the Pincushion's shoulders, pats the man's chest, and looks him winsomely in the eye. "And every word is still true! We've had some grand adventures, haven't we? You've seen new places, met interesting people, been paid well for easy work."

The Pincushion seems to melt in his seat. "Well, yes, in a sense," he mumbles, "but I—it just seems—"

"Now," Kody interrupts again, "if you'd like to leave, I won't stop you. You're free to go any time you like." He turns to look forward again, and both men sit and look for a moment at the low windswept grasses that stretch empty before them in the early winter light. There is no sign anywhere of shelter or comfort.

The Pincushion withdraws the needle from his ear. "No," he says, "I didn't mean—I don't want to leave. Sorry —I suppose I'm just nervous."

Kody pats him again and tells him not to worry. Then the two of them sit in an uncomfortable silence until the Pincushion says, "Um, I'm not sure I can get down while we're still moving. Could you...?"

Kody sighs in his mind and reins in his horse. Behind him the other wagons stop as well, and the creaks and shuffling of travel give way to the empty sound of the low wind. "It's time we stopped to eat anyway," he says as he hops down. Even with the wagon stopped, the Pincushion eases himself to the ground. Kody circles in front of the horse and gives it a pat on its flank. He helps to steady the Pincushion, to whom he says, "Thank you for coming to me. It's important." And though the Pincushion shows him a grateful smile, Kody's patience is wearing thin.

★★★

The Pincushion knows he should be hungry, but he is almost too nervous to eat. As such he is among the last to join the line that leads to the back of the wagon where the food is stored. A voice behind him says, "You seem un-well."

He starts, but when he turns it's only Andra. "It's the salt fish," he complains. "It's practically all we've eaten ever since—well, it's all we've had for weeks, and it doesn't agree with me."

"I miss him, you know. Jorg. Were you close with him?"

They shuffle forward in line. "No, not as such. But it

is unsettling, isn't it? To see that happen to a man."

"We just have to hope that he's in a better place now," Andra says, and she smiles in a way that makes the Pincushion think that she knows something he does not. "Just as we have to hope," Andra adds, "that all of us can one day be in a better place."

The Pincushion doesn't know how to respond to such aphoristic conversation, and so the two of them say nothing more until they're handed their plates of salt fish and bread. They eat sitting on a large waist-high stone nearby. The food is cold in their mouths and the day is cold around them. After a few bites, the Pincushion says, "It's not just Jorg. Those people in that last town—they hated us, didn't they? And now Glyn is gone, too, and Mister Kody seems unhappy, and maybe it's just the short days and the weather that are making me say this—but are we in trouble?"

Andra stops eating and sets her plate down gently on the rock so as to turn her full attention to him. "How do you mean?" she asks.

"It's just," the Pincushion says, and he gestures about himself helplessly, "all of this, does it feel right to you? When I met Mister Kody he seemed so glamorous. But, if we're honest, this isn't glamorous, is it? It's a dangerous, disreputable way to live, and on top of that it might not even last."

As he talks, sadness rises like heat to his cheekbones and his forehead. He is distressed at the strength of his own feeling. Andra reaches out to hold his hand, to give him some measure of softness, but he twitches away from her and stands and rubs his eyes. "Sorry," he says, "I'm sorry—I shouldn't, it's not..." He swallows and takes a breath and tries again. "I should go on patrol. Thank you for—well, you know. Sorry."

He returns his plate to the commissary wagon and trudges towards the rise that lies some few hundred yards ahead of where the Show has stopped. His patrols mean nothing, and he knows as much. He has no skill in letters or numbers, so he can't work with signage, ticketing, or commerce. Kody had at first assigned him to galley duty, but the Pincushion had dropped a stack of plates his second day. He had been barred from tending the horses when he tore one of their feedbags, and had been likewise dismissed from assembling the concession stands when he spilled a bag of fine sugar. Finally, Kody had asked him to protect the Show by guarding its perimeter. Yet for all of his deficiencies, the Pincushion is no fool. He knows full well that he would be helpless in the face of any threat and, therefore, that his vigils protect the Show only insofar as they keep him away from anything valuable or fragile.

Still, he does not complain. His make-believe patrols give him solitude, which he has found to be a blessed rarity in the Show. As he walks up the rise he turns to see the wagon train behind and below him. In its smallness, he feels an invitation to return to himself. The day, he realizes, is almost tender. Its cold air shivers him gently from inside his chest, and its grasses are slightly brittle under his feet. By the time the Pincushion crests the hillock, his worries are distant.

In that moment, breathing hard under the broad ice-blue sky with the Show blocked from view, he steps onto flat ground and sees the forest. Past its border there is only darkness, as though the forest were a fortress built as an act of contumacy against the rule of daylight. The breath-like sway of its leaves and bony bend of its branches evoke for the Pincushion memories of great beasts from childhood tales: the leviathan, the ziz, the behemoth. He stands motionless, as transfixed as any hypnotist's mark.

Distantly, it occurs to him that fear would be the most apt response. Yet somehow he is not afraid. In fact, he is smiling as he walks towards the forest.

At the treeline, the Pincushion hesitates. He holds out one hand as though there might be some tangible energy or resonance that demarcates the bright external world from the forest's recesses—as though the dark itself might be home to some latent power into which the Pincushion could tap. But there is no such barrier, and he enters the forest unimpeded.

Inside, he feels as if he is in a different world. There is a slow and deep stillness in the forest. Sounds there seem to curl toward him only to refract into silence, as though both he and the forest are under a water whose surface is now and again broken. He passes over fragrant pine needles, soft humus, and decay. Far above him, the canopy whispers litanies to itself.

Here, the Pincushion understands for the first time why the people of the capital venerate trees—and that the specific nature of their exaltation is a fallacy. Like the Imperials, every bough yearns to touch the heavens and the blaze of the holy sun that resides therein. Yet the excellence a branch achieves by its reach is made possible only by the grace of the roots below. It is the world of the forest's leafy shadow, he realizes, that is truly divine.

As he contemplates this new theology, the Pincushion comes upon a flowering tree. It stands only slightly taller than he does. Its trunk and branches are a subdued gray-white and its petals are so purely white that they nearly luminesce in the daytime dusk of the forest. The Pincushion is so taken by this tree that he does not notice the soft approaching footsteps, though he does hear the voice that follows.

"Greetings to you, newcomer. Welcome to the land

of the Ufilo."

The Pincushion sees across from him a tall, kind-eyed man wearing a tan-colored robe that is fastened with cloth buttons knotted into elegant designs. The robe is long and sleeveless, and the man is so pale that he seems almost ethereal, as though he were the spirit of the tree given material shape. As he looks more closely, the Pincushion sees that there are points at the tips of the man's ears and a soft chlorophyll undercast to his skin. When the man extends his hand and introduces himself as Nepheli, the Pincushion feels the solidity of him, and he knows that this Nepheli is no vision or apparition.

"It's a pleasure to meet you," the Pincushion says, "I'm the Human Pin—" He stops and blushes. "That is, my name is Piri."

"The pleasure is mine, Piri," Nepheli says. "You must be far from your home. And a lone traveler, as well. Do you have need of food or a place to rest?"

The Pincushion waves both of his hands to ward off the misunderstanding. "No, no, I'm—well, you may be right that I'm far from home, but I'm not alone. I'm part of a traveling circus. Kobold Kody's Show? Maybe you've heard of us?"

Nepheli shakes his head and smiles, and the amusement in his eyes spreads to the Pincushion and relaxes him. "We receive little news of the world outside," Nepheli explains, "but I am glad to learn that you're not alone. Are you here to perform for us? We have little in the way of money, but there are other payments that we can offer."

"Ah, I don't really—" the Pincushion says, and he takes a step back. "I'm not sure if Mister Kody will want to come all the way in here. And there's the money thing, too. But thank you. Anyway, I should be getting back." He holds up a hand in farewell and takes another step away, and as he does so the tree seems to dim. "Goodbye—it really was nice to meet you."

"Goodbye," Nepheli answers. As the Pincushion turns to leave, he sees Nepheli approach the white tree and touch its trunk as though placing a hand on the shoulder of an old friend.

***

The Pincushion arrives back at the Show and sees the garishly painted wagons and feels as though he has not seen them for many years. For a moment, he stands at a remove and watches the horses rouse themselves and strain against their yokes to set the Show in motion again. Kody walks back and forth alongside the slow-moving wagon train checking that nothing is out of place. When he notices the Pincushion, he waves him over and says, "Thought we'd lost you there for a moment, my friend! I was just about to come find you. How'd the patrol go?"

As though he were a string-cut kite tumbling to earth, the Pincushion comes back to himself. He joins Kody, matching his easy walking pace, and says, "There's a forest up ahead. I, um, I met someone there."

Kody's eyes sharpen. "What kind of someone?"

"Oh, he was very kind. He asked me if I was alone and offered to help me. When I said that I was with the Show, he asked if we'd perform for him and his people."

"He tell you who those people were?"

The Pincushion frowns with the effort of remembering. "The Ufilo? I think?"

Now it is Kody who stops and stares. "You met an elf? And the elf asked you to *perform?*" He laughs, delighted and amazed. "Well, why not, then? I'd guess they probably don't have much in the way of money, but I'd wager we can work something out."

The Pincushion nods. "Yessir, Mister Kody, that's just what he said." He has no knowledge of why his meeting would have occasioned such a reaction from the show-master, but he finds his thoughts slewing gently back to the dark forest, the bright tree, and the kindness of Nepheli's touch.

★★★

Kody leads the Show to the edge of the forest. There he gathers Andra and the others together. "I know it seems a little silly to stop again so soon," he says, "but trust me when I say this isn't a chance we're likely to get again. Our good Pincushion here tells me that the elves of this forest have asked us to perform for them, and that's what I intend to do."

Zula shakes out her red hair with one hand and then crosses her arms and says, "Why? They live in a forest and no one ever sees them. Is their money really worth that much more than what we could get in a city?"

"To be perfectly honest with you, I doubt they even have money," Kody answers. "I don't know that they approve of the, well, of the concept, I suppose. But trust me—what they do have'll be worth our while."

Andra thinks immediately of her first vision and the artifacts arrayed between herself and Pol. Two of them are hers already. She wonders if the elves might have a third. In all her travels she's learned little about them. Her visions have shown her nothing of them at all. She only knows that they hold themselves apart from the Empire, neither submitting to it nor confronting it. Of their magics, practices, arts, and doctrines, she is entirely ignorant.

"It had better be worth our while," Zula says. "This Show needs help. It doesn't have much of a future if its biggest attractions keep dropping out. Frankly, aside from me, I don't know why anybody would care to see us at all. But I suppose it's your Show. If we're going in, let's go on in and get it over with."

Kody holds up a sheepish hand. "I'm afraid you won't be coming with us, my dear," he says. "It'll just be me, Etain, Andra, and our friend the Pincushion. Don't get me wrong, Zula, I respect the hell out of you and your talents, you know I do. But we're going to be performing in a forest. It's one thing to use your magic in our tent or out in the open, but I myself would prefer not to have you inadvertently set fire to a falling leaf and burn us all alive."

"Fine," Zula tells him. "I have my own projects to work on anyway. If your elves don't come through for you, Kody, just know that I'm the one who's working on a real solution."

He smiles. "I will most certainly bear that in mind, and I thank you kindly for it. Now," he says, and he looks to the Pincushion as he extends one arm towards the forest, "lead the way."

The Pincushion takes two steps towards the treeline, stops abruptly, and walks back, flustered. "My pins," he says. The eyes of the whole Show are on him as he shuffles to the wagon that holds his possessions to retrieve the rolled waxed canvas that holds the tools of his trade. He slings it over his shoulder, and then he, Kody, Andra, and Etain set out into the forest.

Once the four of them are out of earshot, Kody apologizes on Zula's behalf. "I know she has strong opinions," he says, "but she means well. And I want you all to know that I value each of you. The Show wouldn't be the same without you."

Etain and Andra speak their thanks and their re-assurances, but the Pincushion says nothing.

As they walk, Andra falls back with Etain and quietly asks, "Are you alright?"

"Hm?" Etain says without taking her eyes from the uneven ground. "Oh. Yes, I'm fine. This is unusual, but I'm sure we'll be fine."

Andra sees a root in her path and steps over it carefully. She follows it with her eyes and finds that it belongs to a tree that is wider across than three of the Show's wagons. Its immensity stills her for a moment. Then she says, "That's not what I meant. I know that you and Glyn were friends. Will you be alright without him?"

Etain looks at Andra, though only for an instant. "I don't know," she replies. "I think so. Maybe." With her right hand she rubs one eye and then the other. When Andra reaches out for that same hand, she feels Etain's tears on it.

In time, they find the white tree. Nepheli is waiting for them there. Kody greets the elf with his usual affectation of enthusiasm and introduces him to his performers, and within moments they are following Nepheli deeper into the forest.

They hear the Ufilo village before they see it. There is a wood hammer driving a wooden peg or post, distant laughter, the shift of a pestle. They pass vines that have been pleached into treeside lanterns, their stalks formed into traceries and filigrees. Inside the lanterns, lichen bioluminesce. As they walk further, the lanterns are placed higher and higher on the tree trunks, and the visitors' eyes are drawn upwards to the village proper. A hundred or more feet above the ground they see aqueducts fed by spiraling columns of leaves, bark opening into treeside cleits, constellations of glowing lamps, branchborne walkways, an arboreal cathedral, and more.

Andra marvels at the elvish city. Its construction is unlike anything she knows: neither a conquest of the land nor a grudging compromise with it but something more like a partnership. *Is this some inborn elfin talent,* she wonders, *or is it a result of their magics?* She sees no signs of livestock, such as would attest to the use of sorcery or spellworking, but she also cannot persuade herself to see the elves' tree-lofted world as being a purely mechanical triumph.

"Welcome," Nepheli says before Andra can settle her thoughts. "Please, follow me." They ascend a hanging ladder of stripped branches and woven vines. At the top they find a depository of sorts. There are woven dossers, thick gloves, simple spades, and other tools for transporting goods to and from the forest floor. Among these items stand a number of elves. The eldest among them still carry themselves youthfully, and the youngest wear a maturity beyond their years. All of the men and women are dressed in the same simple robe that Nepheli wears, and all of them have small points at the tips of their ears and pale skin enlivened by a breath of jade.

Nepheli introduces them as Louludi, Risa, Kyma, Stala, and Aelas. Kody shakes hands with each in turn, then beams at his host and says, "Friend Nepheli, I am very grateful indeed to have been invited into this beautiful home of yours. I'm truly honored that you'd ask us here to perform for you. What say you and me have a little chat and let these folks get to know each other better? I always say that the Show looks better when you know who's in it."

Nepheli smiles back. "Gladly, friend Kody," he replies, and the two of them wander to the far edge of the platform, deep in conversation.

The elf woman called Stala waits until they're some distance off and then says, "We've never had traveling performers here before. What is it that you do?"

"I'm a human pincushion," the Pincushion says.

"What is that?"

"I—er, well," the Pincushion starts, "I can stab myself. Without harm, I mean."

He fears that he has made himself ridiculous, but the elves look at him only with mild confusion. "And you?" Stala asks of Etain.

"I'm a contortionist," she says. "I can bend my body in unusual ways."

"And I'm a seer," Andra adds.

"Ah," Aelas, a boy, says, "then will you tell me my fortune?"

"Perhaps," she says in her stage voice. "Perhaps. The gift cannot be commanded, only heeded. But I will try." Quickly she decides on a gamble. She holds out a hand towards him and closes her eyes. "I see," she says, "a scale belonging to an ancient beast. I see a box of fire. What do you know of those things?"

Louludi chuckles, and all turn to her. She is the oldest among them by far, and she chews patiently on a piece of a five-pointed leaf. "We know nothing of the concerns of your world," she says, "and that is as it should be." Her voice creaks like the trees themselves. "I know you humans. You take your powers from the animals who live under the sky and are ruled over by Sol. He is a powerful god, and he has made you powerful! But there are many gods.

"Look around you," she continues. "The gods of seed and branch shelter us. Their enchantments grow slow and strong, green and gray. The light of your sun god can't penetrate here. Neither can his sight." She smiles and takes another small bite from her leaf. "If it's a vision you're after, you'll have to get by with your eyes like the rest of us."

Before Andra can respond, Kody returns, smiling and holding a palm-sized cloth bag that is cinched at the top. He hefts the bag once as if to reassure himself of its weight, then drops it in a pocket on the inside of his coat. "Well," he says to his cast, "I'd say we have ourselves a deal. What do you say we give these people what they paid for?"

***

Before the Pincushion performs, he asks Louludi for some of her leaf. He doesn't know what it is and he doesn't ask. He only knows that he wants to try it, that there is something in the elves that he wants to emulate or adopt for his own. She tears off a leaf tip and hands it to him without hesitation or judgment. "Chew it patiently," she tells him. "Even for your first time, its effects will be slow."

He does chew it patiently, first during their procession to the wide platform that will serve as their stage and then throughout Kody's opening monologue and Etain's act. He chews, and he swallows the virid pulp; and as he does, his mind slows. Before his eyes the sparse daylight floats up through the treetops and is replaced with glowlights of all sizes and colors. Etain in particular seems to him to move with a keen and aching slowness, her limbs wordlessly encoding some ancient sylvan guidance. He watches her with an unreasoning joy: Etain in midair, sequined and tree-held; Etain, focusing and focused on; Etain, branch-slender, languid as a reed in the breeze, confidante of the susurrant dusk.

The Pincushion is not in love. He is simply at peace. Whether through magic or medicine, the elven herb has taken the burden of self-knowledge from him. He looks out at the world without formulating any plan of action or activity; he smiles and does not know he is smiling. Only when he stands to take Etain's place onstage, and feels the same verdant slowness in himself, does he understand that the leaf is in his blood.

With the return of understanding, his thousand minor agonies return as well. Yet the leaf has not left him, and it causes his own familiar sentiments to echo strangely within him. On the stage he selects a slender pin and holds it up for the audience's inspection and watches for their response. The elves don't react as humans would. They show no horror or helpless fixation or glee. From the balconies and windows of treeside houses, pairs and trios of Ufilo watch him intently, as though he has some vital lesson to teach. The larger groups at the edges of the platform stage look at him with sadness in their eyes. As for the children among them, the Pincushion finds that he cannot meet their eyes.

Slowly, he brings the needle to his ribs. He watches it to ensure that it catches the light. When the moment is right, he presses it through his skin and muscle until it passes in between his lung and his stomach and exits the other side of his body.

Someone makes a small sound of sympathy and sorrow. He looks up to trace it, but it was not an elf. It was the Pincushion himself. Suddenly he feels the loneliness of being onstage, of being set in a circle of light, isolated from the ones who watch from the safety of the dark. He selects another needle. His hands no longer feel like his own. *Why are you doing this to me?* he asks his hands. *Why are you doing this?* Their response is to stab him again: through the left shoulder, through the right calf, through the center of his palm.

The pain is not new. Although he never bleeds or retains any mark of his wounds, he has always felt the slide of the cold metal through his body and suffered every prick. But Louludi's leaf has changed the pain for him. Now it is unbearable, not in its intensity but in its evitability. The elves in his audience are holding each other with tenderness, with care, with pleasure; they're leaning on one another familiarly, casually; each is rooted in every other. As he stands in their midst and pins himself to the air, he sees that he is rooted nowhere and to no one.

He finishes his act to thoughtful applause and withdraws the needles one by one from his own body. *It could be different*, he thinks. *Everything could be different.* Piri places the needles back in their places in his tool roll. He knows he will never take them out again.

Andra takes the stage next, but he doesn't watch. Instead he seeks out Nepheli among the crowd. In a whisper he asks if he can stay and live among the Ufilo. Nepheli moves to embrace him, and he remembers Kody's proprietary arm around his shoulder and stiffens. But Nepheli's hold on him is as warm and deep as the scent of spring. "Welcome, brother," the elf whispers back.

After the abbreviated Show concludes, the crowd begins to disperse and Etain approaches him. "You were amazing," she says. "I don't know what you changed, but it felt so different to watch you tonight."

"You were, too," he replies, and lifts his head to the darkened roof of branches above. "I think it's this place."

Etain looks up as well. But he can tell that she does not understand, that to her the trees are only trees. "Maybe," she says politely. "But you really were special. I've watched your act before, but I think this was the first time I really saw you. I couldn't stop wondering which magics you use."

"Magic?" he replies. "I have no magic. Who would want to give themselves this power?"

"But then how can you...?"

"I don't know. I just can. Ever since I was young. Some friends—or, some of the other children, anyway—they, ah. They discovered it one day. They used a sewing needle. At first I was afraid, but there was no blood, no scar. And from then on, there was something special about me. I liked that. It's the only real talent I've ever had. It makes people look at me like I shine—like you're looking at me now." He smiles sadly. "There aren't many chances to have someone look at you like that.

"That's why I joined the Show. I saw how the people in my village looked at you. How they looked at Zula and Andra and Glyn. And Jorg. I thought this was my chance. I could do what I was meant to do. I could use this, well, this thing that made me special. I could make it my livelihood. But I don't think I want that anymore."

Before Etain can reply, they hear loud bootsteps on the wood platform and Kody interrupts them.

"Have you two seen Andra?" he asks. "I've just about had as much fun as I can have up here and I figure I'm ready to get back."

"I'm not going," Piri says.

"You're what?"

He meets Kody's eyes as best he can. "I'm staying here with the Ufilo, Mister Kody. I want to live with them."

Kody sighs and slides his hat back and scratches his head. "Well, I guess that's up to you, but are you sure? You don't exactly know these people."

"You always said I was free to go whenever I wanted

to, didn't you? Now I want to."

For a moment or two Kody doesn't move. Then he pulls his hat back down on his head and his eyes go hard and he pats the Pincushion on the shoulder one last time. "Fair enough," he says. "But if you'll excuse me, I need to find my fortuneteller. Come on, Etain."

Kody turns to locate Andra, but Etain hesitates. "I'm sorry," she says. "That you want to go, I mean. We'll miss you."

"You could stay," he replies. "You could all stay."

She shakes her head and looks towards her ringmaster, dark and impatient among the gathered elves. "I can't leave him. I know that it feels like everything is ending. But I want to be there when it does. I owe him that much."

"Then I wish you all good things," Piri says. "May the light shine on you—and the dark as well."

She takes one step towards him and pauses, as though he were a fearful animal who might at any moment turn and run. When she sees that he won't, she hugs him, and he hugs her in return.

Soon Kody calls and waves from across the platform. He has found Andra. It is time to leave.

Piri watches them go. He readies himself for some press of emotion: the sadness of leaving a friend, the withering fear of disappointing a colleague. He finds neither. In their place, there is only a pale green shoot, unfurling peacefully in the dark.

III: The Contortionist

From the edge of the elven forest, the Show travels due south towards Harold's homeland. The season cools further. In the mornings, the ground is frost-covered and hard. For the first time in her life, Etain feels the cold underneath her skin. The Show is no longer the enclosure it once was for her. Now it is a punctured vessel, a shredded tent open to the air. From its remote heights above her, the sun warms her skin but provides no deeper comforts.

Halfling territory announces itself modestly, not by monuments or gateways but by a gentle and gradual grooming of the land itself. Etain is briefly charmed by the gold-lit orchards and vineyards through which the Show's wagons pass, but she saddens again when they enter the village proper. The houses and workshops there are no taller than she is; the Show wagons overtop them easily. Etain looks at them and cannot help but see more of Kody's fakery. In her eyes, they take on the aspect of a cleverly worked trick of perspective or some cunning stagecraft.

As the rest of her party greet Harold's kin and exchange pleasantries, she retreats to a nearby field and stretches herself in all directions until the sound of her own breath calms her. *Just think of something else*, she tells herself, *something pleasant*. But the only pleasure she can bring to mind is hundreds of miles away on the northern coast.

The halflings welcome her and her colleagues with open arms but do not accept Kody's offer to perform. "We don't believe in the practice of acquiring and using magics," Harold explains. "But stay! Stay the night! We've come at just the right time to celebrate the harvest."

★★★

The next day is devoted entirely to a single hours-long feast: bacon and corncakes, spiced eggs, gamefowl stuffed with herbs, juices and wines, buttered potatoes, flour dumplings in a sweet broth, roasted carrots and beets, dark bread and light biscuits, tarts, pastries, and berries. Andra eats and watches the laughter on the small faces and hopes that the Empire will continue to leave the halflings in peace.

She doesn't know why they've been left alone until now. She also knows how little the reason matters. When the Empire drove itself east, it won only parched soil and bloodied hands. When Pol cursed her, he gained nothing at all. Andra knew, even as a child of the Empire, that magic could be a weapon. Now she knows that there are people for whom a weapon's use is a self-ratifying thing, not bound or conditioned by the niceties of rational con-sideration. They are the halflings' opposites. They may be Andra's opposites as well.

Nestled amid the halflings' guilelessness and merry-making, she thinks ahead to her destiny with Pol, and for the first time she is relieved to know that the four weapons in her vision are not weapons after all. *Whatever happens,* she thinks with a cup of cider warming her hands, *at least I won't end up like him.*

The feast concludes at dusk. After the tables are cleared, the halflings and the Show members converse by candlelight deep into the night. Andra asks again after the ancient scale and a box of fire. Again she finds neither. In the morning, the Show departs. Harold stays.

★★★

With so many of the Show's members now gone, its days become little more than cyclical successions of self-renewing assignments. Andra cooks and cleans and washes. Coner and Lady Ugok lift and push what needs to be lifted or pushed. Zula takes up hunting and sequesters herself in her wagon to advance a project whose nature she will not discuss.

Etain, handy with tools from her starveling miner's childhood, becomes the Show's jack-of-all-trades. In this way, her thoughts of Glyn bleach and fade under the glare of continuous labor. She patches tents that are torn in Coner's haste or in their patrons' drunkenness. She fletches new arrows for Kody's marksman act. She shoes the horses and prepares their feedbags. When the Show travels far enough south that the ground turns rocky and they spot an outlying dwarven trading post on the horizon, Etain effects repairs on the Show's durable goods so as to ready them for sale.

"Don't try to make 'em good as new or anything like that," Kody explains to her. "We don't need 'em to be perfect—just good enough that those stingy bastards'll pay us a good price."

So she threads herself through wagon undercarriages, wrench in hand; and she oils scenery joints that have been clogged by the accumulated dust of a continent; and as task stacks upon task she thinks of herself more and more as a mechanical thing incapable of feeling. In this she finds some relief. That night she falls asleep oblivious to her surroundings, thinking neither of the many things that are near to her nor the one who is far.

The following morning is a tunnel of light. Clouds sheath the sky from horizon to horizon but only spread its brightness without decreasing it. Pale rocks jut from the ground and reflect the milky sky with an intensity that makes Etain's eyes ache. Kody gathers the remnants of his Show together over their breakfasts and finally addresses the fears they've carried unspoken for months.

"We've gone through a lot of change," he says. "A lot of change. And that's scary. Jorg, Glyn, Jack and all them, our friend the Pincushion, now Harold—almost seems like the sun is setting on us. But they do say it's darkest just before the dawn, and I believe a new dawn is coming for this Show."

Etain's worries redouble. She has heard speeches of this sort before back in the mines. She knows they do not end well.

"Then why are we selling most of it off?" Coner asks, his scales dulled by anger.

"That's a superb question. As I said, a new day is coming, and the Show will again rise. I intend to sell only what we don't need and use the funds to build a new Show, a better Show." Kody pauses. Etain realizes that he's speaking in his stage patter, as though they're neither his partners nor his allies but his marks. Zula leans forward with a kindle of enthusiasm that lights her eyes.

But Coner slams his bowl against the ground so that the spoon rattles inside it, and he stands and says, "And let me guess: for this new Show of yours, you won't be needing us."

"I do confess that I hadn't fully worked out all the details," Kody says quickly, then holds out his palms and continues, "But! But! You've all been loyal and kind to me. I promise that I fully intend to repay your commitment as best I'm able to. Yes, maybe there will be some, ah, diminishment. But you all know my Show has always been a home for people who don't have one, and—"

"And now that home will just 'diminish' a little?" Coner finishes for him. "Go chew glass, you two-bit huckster, you cheap fraud, you—do you really still think we're too stupid to tell the difference between a charity and a get-rich-quick scheme formulated by a moron? I knew this day would come—I knew you'd run out of luck and leave us twisting."

Etain watches them argue with a sickened fascination. She wonders if she, too, is to be cast out. Memory springs up in her like a jack from a box. She smells coal dust and feels her stomach twist and looks for a place to vomit.

Meanwhile Coner takes his small pack of belongings and slings it roughly over his shoulder and points to the dwarven trading post in the distance. "If you want someone to drag your trash all the way out there, you do it yourself. I'm done with you." And with that he is gone, walking back the way they've come.

Kody waits until Coner is out of earshot, then chuckles. Not one of his remaining staff believes that his mirth is genuine. "Well," he begins, but Zula cuts him off.

"Forget him," she says. "He was never irreplaceable. He was nothing and you made him something, and now he's choosing to be nothing again. I'm just glad you're viewing this as an opportunity to be seized, as we talked about. How quick do you think we can turn it around? Because I have a—"

"Later," Kody says. "Let's talk later. Right now I guess I got some trash to take out. Ugok?" he asks.

Zula steps forward. "Don't just push me aside—I can help, too. We can discuss the Show on the way."

"The fewer the better," Kody replies, already in motion. "Dwarves can be..." He makes an ambiguous sound and turns his back on Zula. Within minutes, he and Lady Ugok and four of the Show's six horsedrawn wagons are on the way to the dwarves.

The three women watch them go. "I hope he gets a good price," Etain says.

Andra pats her arm. "He will. If anyone can out-haggle a dwarf, it's Kody. But you," she says to Zula, "I never knew you had plans for the Show. What are they? More magic?"

"And why should I tell you?" Zula says, and she takes a step towards Andra. "I've seen how you cozy up to him. This new Show of his—I'd bet my life's earnings that it's not his idea at all. How long ago did you whisper it into his ear? At the harvest festival? With the elves, where you knew I couldn't overhear you? Did you tell him that you'd seen it in one of your 'visions'? You may have everyone else fooled, Andra, but not me."

She waits for Andra to return her challenge, but Andra says nothing. After a moment's hesitation Zula shakes her head, turns, and walks away, closing her hands here and there upon the tall brambles that reach from between the rocks, leaving ash behind.

"Are you—?" Etain begins timidly.

"Never mind me," Andra sighs. "Someone has to clean these dishes. Would you like to help?"

Together they gather up the bowls and the flatware and walk down to a nearby stream. Etain sits at the bank with crossed legs. Andra kneels carefully to join her. In doing so, she sees that Etain's breakfast is still mostly un-touched. "Etain, you must eat. I know times have been hard, but you have to keep your strength up."

Etain smiles sadly. "Strength?" she asks. "I've never been the strong one. I'm the flexible one. I'm the one who adapts."

"Please, Etain. If not for yourself then for me."

Etain feels a flash of anguish like a sunbolt that breaks

through cloud cover for a moment and is swallowed up again. For Andra, she finishes her breakfast. She tastes none of it, and the dishes likewise have no texture or temperature in her hands as she washes them.

"What's holding your thoughts?" Andra asks her as she works.

Etain sets the bowl in her hands onto the ground and shrugs and tries to pitch her voice so that it will be stable. "The mines, I suppose. From—before."

Andra tends to her washing. "Why? Those days are far behind you."

"What if they're in front of me, too?" Etain asks. "Jack used to say that there was an ocean at the beginning of the world and that there will be an ocean at its end. Maybe that's the way it is with me and the mines. Kody himself said the Show will be changing. Now Zula is causing trouble. What will I do if the Show goes away and I have nothing else?"

"Oh, child," Andra says. At last she sets down her washing and turns to Etain. "The end of the Show is not the end of the world."

Harold, the Pincushion, and Glyn, all of them have gone happily and freely to better lives. But Etain's mind is still trapped below the earth. "There was no room," she says, "in the mines. No space to breathe. We were always hot, so close to one another. They put torches on the walls with sun-shaped backplates that shone so bright I could barely look at them. We moved rocks for hours and hours, and to make us work harder they told us that the longer we stayed under the light the more Sol would favor us. They said shirkers would stay in the darkness forever.

"But the dark was the only relief I had. We would leave the mines at night and the air was so sweet, so cool. The whole aboveground world was so beautifully dark and safe. I could close my eyes and imagine I was anywhere."

"And where did you imagine you were?" Andra asks.

Etain shrugs her shoulders as if in preparation for a blow or a harsh word. "With someone strong, someone who would hold me and protect me even at his own cost," she says in a child's small voice. "With someone who— someone who lo—"

But she can't say the word. Andra rises and goes to her. She sits alongside Etain and softly pulls Etain's head to her shoulder and waits while Etain trembles.

The sound of Etain's breathing is a sadness, but the sound of the stream beside them is a comfort. Andra remembers Loloudi's claims about other gods and the story the old barbarian woman told her in her hometown: the story of the gods who were banished below the waves and who now speak only in the whispers trapped inside seashells. Andra places one hand in the water and prays to the gods of the rill that her voice should be a comfort as well.

"Don't be so sad," she says in a voice like water. "After all, we know someone who fits that description." She puts a hand on Etain's cheek and tilts her head up so that she can look in her eyes. Then she smiles and says, "It's just not Kody, is all."

Etain smiles, then laughs, and then she is silent. Andra releases her and quickly finishes cleaning the dishes. The two of them linger under the pale-bright sky, Andra watching the shadows of thoughts pass over Etain's face like the shadows of greater or lesser birds winging over the earth.

Etain does not notice the attention paid to her. She is lost in contemplation of the runlet beside which they sit. It's a small thing, hardly more than two feet wide, and entirely clear but for where it twirls and juggles the light. Etain has seen any number of such streams during her travels, but this one seems almost to call to her, and in the manner of one dreaming she realizes that she understands this stream, that she knows it in the way she knows herself. The land may appear to hold the stream in its grip, as circumstances seem to constrain Etain herself. Creatures of all sorts may unthinkingly use the stream for their various purposes, as the miners and Kody have used her for theirs. Yet the stream belongs to none of them and can be possessed by none of them, for it always and forever flows beyond them to its home.

She wakes from this dream of understanding and stands. Andra stands as well, bowls and spoons in hand, and makes as if to return to the wagons. But Etain only takes off her necklace and asks Andra to wait.

"You're right," Etain says. One hand is clasped against her breastbone, the string dangling from it. "There is someone who will love me if I go to him. Kody did well by me in his way, but I don't belong in his Show anymore." She smiles sadly. "Maybe I never did. And neither do you, Andra," she adds. "So come with me. Glyn will be happy to see you—I know he will. And the two of us will have an easier journey together than I would alone."

Andra grins a lopsided grin. "It's so much like you to think of me even now," she tells Etain. "Thank you. But no —I can't leave. Not yet."

"I thought you might say that." Etain steps forward and presses her necklace into Andra's free hand. The charm is rough and keeled and nearly as thin as a fingernail, and it is as black as night. She turns it over in her hand and Etain says, "I heard you, you know. When you were talking to the elves and the halflings. I don't know why I didn't give it to you sooner."

The object is as wide as Andra's palm and cold to the touch. She turns it over curiously and asks, "But what is it?"

"A scale," Etain says, "from an ancient creature who lived deep, deep underground." Andra looks up sharply, but Etain doesn't pause to let her speak. "We found it in the mines one day. We had taken so much coal out from the earth that there seemed to be none left, but the proprietors demanded more. The adults were sent to make fresh shafts. After some time they broke into one end of a curved tunnel that was already there. It was twice as tall as ours, and the far end, two hundred feet away or more, was blocked by fallen dirt and rock.

"No one knew how it had come to be there. It was tiled all around, walls and ceiling and floor, but nobody had mined that area before. We were all fascinated by what the adults had found. Within hours we were telling fables and spreading rumors of ancient civilizations and lost empires, but the overseers came down and scolded us for our idleness and told the adults to get back to digging. When they tried to break through the tiles, their picks and shovels just bounced off. After hours of effort they managed to pry a few of them loose, but they never even so much as scratched the others. Eventually they gave up and went to clear the debris from the far end. When they did, they saw that the tiles ended there."

Andra looks at the scale in her hand, then back at Etain.

"That's right," Etain says. "They weren't tiles after all. They were the scales of something called a wurm, left behind when it molted. We only found out after the owners of the mine called in specialists from the Imperial Academy. At first we thought we'd found a treasure trove —imagine the magics hiding in the body of such a huge, powerful creature! But the scholars said that the scales were impervious to human manipulation. So the mine owners just ordered us to work around the remains of the wurm, as though it was any other obstruction. Even though the scales were useless, a few of us took one just for the sake of having a new thing.

"And until now, that was the end of it." Etain shrugs and smiles. "Because now I know I was meant to have it so I could give it to you."

Andra stands still. For a moment, she is speechless. Then she puts the scale into her pocket and smiles and says, "Come on—let's get back to the wagons and put these dishes away so I can hug you and thank you properly."

★★★

Kody returns alone later that evening. A ribbon of purple smoke unspools in lazy swaths from a pipe that few of his employees have ever seen him use. The taste of the smoke is ancient and sweet, a fitting gift from the elves. It lifts up his spirits and lightens his stride.

When he draws near he sees a number of human strangers sitting with his employees around the campfire. Kody is unsurprised. Such chance meetings of unrelated groups are common enough on the road. These travelers have the simple clothes and broad shoulders of builders and craftspeople, but their gestures are as grand and expansive as any potentate's and their laughter carries in the twilight. Even a hundred feet away and through the fascinating spell of the pipesmoke, Kody smells money on them. From a distance, he hails them as though they are all old friends.

"That's who we were telling you about," Etain tells them. "That's Kody. But—Kody, where's Lady Ugok?"

"Gone," Kody says, still a silhouette against the cooling night sky. "Gone, gone. She's staying with the dwarves. Apparently she spoke dwarf this whole time—who knew!"

He steps into the light, and the leader of the group of strangers stands and calls Kody's name and holds his arms wide. In one hand he holds a bottle of liquor. With the other he takes Kody and embraces him. Soon the two of them are sitting around the fire with the rest and bantering like two roughcast characters in a stage play.

"These fine ladies tell me you're a showman!" the leader bawls. "Not much of a show, though, is it? Just the four of you?"

Kody winks at him with the exaggerated slowness of the inebriate, though he is more controlled than he lets on. "My officers in the army always told me," he answers, "that the size of the man in the fight mattered less than the size of the fight in the man."

As he speaks, Kody takes them in. Men and women alike have close-cut hair, rough hands, and strong backs. He sees their mule sketched some ways beyond the fire-light, and nearby he spies a cart that he imagines contains the various tools and implements of their respective trades. He considers taking them in a rigged game of chance or goading them into purchasing a performance or some of his many useless elixirs. But there is gentleness in the falling dark, and the lilac-colored smoke coils weight-lessly inside his ribs, and he decides to let them be.

"Well," one of the women in the group says, "I've not yet met a man who had enough fight for me, but who knows—maybe you'll be the first." While her comrades laugh, she grins a wolf's grin and reaches for the leader's bottle and takes a swig, then adds, "And your officers can go hang! Emperors die and kingdoms fall, but the Lord of Coins is the one ruler that will live forever. And tonight we are all guests in his court!"

A cheer goes up from the workers. Zula joins them. Kody listens to the sound fly over the land, now in full dark, and gauges the distance of its travel. "I must confess," he says, "that my pleasure on your behalf is somewhat overpowered by concern. These are dangerous lands—aren't you at all worried about announcing your wealth so loudly?"

The workers look at one another bemusedly. "You really were in the army, weren't you, old man?" the leader asks. "I took you for a run-of-the-mill grifter, but there's some honor in you after all."

"Careful," Andra says, "you might hurt his feelings."

Kody laughs along this time. "Yes, I'm afraid it's true—I'm not half the rogue I used to be."

"Nor are these lands half of what they used to be, thanks to you," the leader says, and he claps Kody on the shoulder. "You Imperials made the frontier by pushing your way out here, and then you unmade it by pushing more. Look at how much better the world is now! How much freer we all are!"

"You should see the city that's going up in the south," adds another one of the workers, an older man. "Used to be there were only barbarians and goblins thereabouts. But now! The gardens, the bathhouses—white marble, blonde wood, coppered inlays, glass domes. And the beaches! I'd never seen the like."

Kody hums and points his pipestem towards the worker and exhales smoke. "Why, how interesting! That's precisely where we mean to go. We aim to speak with Pol, the Light of the Sun. We believe," he says with a glance at Andra, "that's where he is."

"Pol?" Zula exclaims. "The poet?" She says the word as though it's the name of some shameworthy disease. "*That's* your new plan for the Show? Poetry?"

Zula's anger is a cheap mask, and Andra sees through it. Zula's dispute with Pol does not stem from his poetry. Fakes and freaks have long been her companions, yet never has she objected to them or their dubious arts. Her spite is in truth a guise for her fears. *Power shared is power lessened*, Pol once told Andra. She wonders now if he meant magic or something else, some vicious capacity to condemn another person to the living extinction of obsolescence. If Andra knew where to find a creature whose guts or bones offered shelter from such desuetude, she would track one down and make of it a gift to Zula. As it is, she can only say, "Pol is more than a poet."

"Why, yes he is indeed!" the old laborer says. "It was Pol who hired us. I tell you now I would have paid money just to say I met the man. The first time we saw him he was out on the ocean just standing on the water. He walked to us straight across the waves, and as he came he sang so beautifully that the fish themselves leapt up to hear. They say he's even older than I am, but he looked as young as spring. He even glowed—and I don't mean that as a figure of speech. Light came off the man like he truly was the sun. I tell you, any single one of his magics would be worth more money than I've seen in my lifetime."

"You've had too much to drink, old-timer," Zula says sourly, throwing a pebble into the fire.

"No," the leader replies, "it's all true, and more. He spoke with the seabirds and called down hailstones from a clear sky so that he could cool his wine before he drank it. When he led us to the site of his home, we learned that the footings had been placed wrong. Pol moved them himself, easy as you please." He pauses and looks at the four remaining constituents of the Show. "I don't mean to offend," he says, "but I doubt whether he'll agree to meet with you—or, if he does, what you'd have to offer a great man like him."

At that Zula stands and snarls. The campfire roars and billows outward and is swept all at once into the sky, where it dwindles to nothing. "You would be better served to ask what he can offer us," she says in the sudden blackness. Then there is the sound of her retreating footsteps.

After a moment, Kody chortles. His pipe clacks lightly between his teeth, and the sound makes him laugh harder. "You'll have to forgive her," he explains to the workers. "Zula is our resident pyromancer. She, ah—she is not shy to make herself understood. I thank you all for the conversation and for keeping my friends company in my absence. But the hour must be awfully late by now and I do believe we might be best served to continue our acquaintance in the light of day." He, too, stands. "Gentlemen, ladies." Kody tips his hat in the dark, and he walks back to the Show wagons.

The workers mutter amongst themselves, but they rise as one and make their unsteady way to their cart so as to find their bedding. Andra also pushes herself up but is held back by Etain. "Andra," she asks quietly, as if to keep her words from reaching the multitudinous audience of stars, "what do you think about...?"

"Ask them," Andra says. "They seem kind enough. And they've come from the south, so surely they're going north some ways. Even if they won't take you all the way to him, it'd be a start."

So it is that, when Kody exits his tent in the gray-blue morning, Etain is packed and waiting for him. She and the workers have already eaten and are dressed for travel. Kody is still bleared from the previous night's pipesmoke, and he wears only his long pajamas. He stands and blinks to clear the sleep from his eyes and scratches his beard. "Well, I've had plenty of 'good mornings' that were also 'goodbyes,'" he says, "but none of them were ever quite like this."

"I'm sorry," Etain says, holding a small valise in front of her with both hands. "You've done so much for me, and now I'm just leaving you. But my heart is—is somewhere else. I hope you can understand."

Something inherent in the tableau before him, some tenderness or solemnity, catches Kody unprepared, and he forgets his usual persona. "Oh, enough of that. I can't think of one thing I did *for* you. I've only undone what others did *to* you, and even then I only undid it partway," he says, and for once he speaks only the truth. He rubs his face with one hand and waves her away with the other. "Go on. I'll be fine. The Show ain't over yet, and I trust that the same light that shines on your travels will shine on the both of us when we meet up again."

Etain wipes a tear from each eye. She nods. And then, to the sound of friendly chatter and creaking wheels, she and the workers and their mule start their voyage north.

Andra and Zula wake at the noise and join Kody to watch the group depart. "You were right again," he says to his seer. "It happened just the way you told me: She left in tears." He sighs, and his breath shakes as he does so. There is so little around him now, so little to insulate him from the indifferent world. In their undisguised paltryness, the two women and the few wagons he has left seem less substantial to him even than the single horse and longknife he was given as a scout. At least there was never a need to pretend the latter were more than they were.

He shakes these thoughts out of his head. For decades now his only expertise has been the perpetuation of pretense. "There's hardly any sense in stopping now," he tells himself out loud. "South we go, to Pol and the golden ocean and the grand reopening of Kobold Kody's Show.

"Who wants breakfast?" he adds tiredly. Andra is already halfway to the wagons to find their food.

But Zula has not moved. "First things first," she says. "You and I need to have a talk."

The Pyromancer & The Poet

I: In A Different Shape

Zula and Kody have their conversation. Then, in the manner of a wooden creature staked to a carousel which spins and spins and goes nowhere, they have it again and again all the way to the southern coast. One morning, Andra is feeding and watering the horses when it starts again. Zula sees Kody pinch a sticky brownblack substance out of the drawstrung bag he received from the elves, and she upbraids him for it.

"My dear Zula," Kody replies, "what is the origin of this hostility? Ah—no, wait, I have it. I promised that I'd give you your share. Here, take as much as you like. I will readily vouch for its salubrious effects." He holds out the bag and smiles loosely.

"How can you do this to yourself?" Zula fiercely replies. "How can you do this to what you've built? The Show needs you now more than ever, and yet here you are, chasing some daydream and numbing yourself with elf-tainted herbs. Look around you, Kody—there's nothing left of us! Our light has gone out!"

"Now, now. Even behind a cloud, the sun still shines,"

Kody says, and he tamps the elven tobacco into his pipe and lights it.

Andra ignores them. She has one hand on a horse's broad flank. When she breathes in, there is the scent of dry oats, sickly-sweet smoke, horse sweat, and the sun on cloth and flesh. She doesn't know how she'll lay her hands on the box of fire. All she knows is that she will. She is ready. She wants to breathe in and smell the sea.

The following day, while Zula and Kody continue their argument, Andra kneels a few feet away and fills a bucket with soil so that she can smother their campfire. Neither of them acknowledge her. Kody has always taken for granted those who worked beneath him. Now Zula has learned to do the same. "Are you still set on throwing away everything you've built?" she asks.

"I'm still intent on shedding those things that have weighed us down," Kody replies. "Like you, I want us to reach even loftier heights. Right now I'm just springing for the leap, is all."

"Ah, yes, your beloved poet. What could possibly make you think that he'd join us? An antique soldier, a fire mage, and a fake fortuneteller—what would we have to offer him?"

Kody looks slyly at Andra, who is still filling her bucket one careful trowelful of soil at a time. She inspects each one for light soil or sand, for any sign that the coast might be near. "I have it on good authority that he'll hear us out," Kody says.

Zula stands and interposes herself between Kody and Andra. "And then what?" she asks. "You approach him and you say what? How do you persuade him, a regular guest at the Imperial court, to be the centerpiece of a run-down traveling circus?"

"Why, Zula, is that how you see us? A mere circus?"

Kody feigns affront. "We've always been more than that. We're a showcase of frontier life, an education imparted through stagecraft and dramaturgy. It's just that our lessons have to change. Those workers back there were right: The frontier is gone now, both in reality and even in the minds of the people. The old Show would never have survived. We would always have needed a new one."

Before Zula can answer, Andra sifts dirt over the glowing ashes of the campfire. Though she already knows what their answers will be, she asks, "Wouldn't a circus be enough? Must we always try to force the Show to outstrip itself, to be larger and grander than it is?" Andra smiles. "I like a circus."

Zula scoffs and walks away in disgust. Kody watches her go, then pats Andra on the shoulder and says, "Getting cold feet? I understand. Change ain't always pretty—I saw it with my own two eyes, so I should know. I know those workers back there made Pol sound awfully impressive. But don't you worry. Like the good sun itself, our Show will rise again, and it'll be better and brighter than ever."

He pats her again, then stands and goes to chart the day's path, leaving Andra alone with her thoughts of what might have been. *Of what might still be*, she reminds herself, *if I can make it that far.*

★★★

Together the three of them move south and south again. Even here the days grow short, and the sun seems always to be rising or setting like a tightrope walker tumbling from one horizon to the other. Over time, they leave the true winter behind them and arrive in a place of clemency. The grasses underfoot become stiff and broad, and the far-spaced trees turn wide and soft. Where moss had been in the north, they find instead flowering vines.

Soon enough they find outlying signs of settlement and civilization. At first there are only scattered and temporary workers' camps, among which Kody stops the Show to play to the populace one last time. Their performance is listless and slipshod. Kody opens the night with his pipe already lit and discovers under its influence that his familiar lines disorient him. Andra reads vague and hackneyed prophecies in the palms of volunteers. Zula, whom Kody advertises as the feature act, enters the circle of onlookers with such seething resentment for him that even the audience is cowed by her.

The Show's final production thus ends in failure, and its principals know why. Though all three appear to have different functions as performers, their true and shared undertaking is to loosen the hold of the world so that their customers can, for a few moments, feel themselves free of its grip. Yet the Show's remnant veterans can only achieve this if they themselves possess a degree of freedom, and tonight they do not. Tonight, oppressed by thoughts of Pol, they are all as nervy as novice street actors startled into stage fright by the stares of passersby.

After they conclude their dud, Zula approaches Kody to make her case one last time. "Do you see now?" she demands of him. "There's no Show left for you to save. It's over, Kody. Don't pretend that pomposity and bombast are the answer."

"I won't have this conversation with you again," Kody answers wearily. He turns away from her, towards the dark and rest, but Zula calls a flame to her hand and follows.

"I'm not the source of the problem," she says, "and you know that. What I am is the source of the solution, if you'll only listen."

Kody turns on his heel to face her. "Fine—fine. I

know a sales pitch when I see one coming. So what exactly is it that you want to sell me?"

Zula smiles. "I thought you'd never ask."

She leads him and Andra back to the wagons, where she searches through her belongings for a plain wooden box that's only slightly longer than her hand and an inch or two high. Andra knows it by sight: it is the box from her first vision, the last of the items with which she will confront Pol. She almost reaches out to take it, but restrains herself. When she does she notices that one long side of the box is covered in a scaly paper of sorts, and she looks to Zula to explain.

"Think," Zula says to them both, "of the Show's full name. No matter what you might say now, Kody, we're not just a circus. We are a Frontier Exposition *and Tonic Show.* Why is that? Because there is a need for magic to descend from the lofty heights of Emperors and Academics—and poets—so that it can be held and enjoyed by all."

"So," Kody says, tired and exasperated, "you want us to take up traveling pharmacology? It can't be done. Imagine if every single person had your powers, Zula. Every criminal, every madman, every power-hungry schemer and rage-filled brute. It would be chaos. It might even be the end of everything we know. Our magics ought to go to those who are deserving, those we can trust. Besides, you know my tonics are all fakes. The real stuff is far too hard to come by."

She sneers at him. "I'm not talking about selling power. I'm talking about selling tools. Watch." At this, she slides the box open to reveal a pile of matches, one of which she removes and ignites against the striking surface on the box's side.

Andra looks at the light for any signs of peculiarity or distinctiveness, but she sees none. The match tip flares pale yellow, then settles into a sharp white. It gives off no abnormal heat, nor does its light travel far enough to draw the neighboring lean-tos and rough-beds out of the dark.

"Yes, Zula, it's a match," Kody says. As he talks he takes his hat off and runs his hand over his hair in frustration. "Now if that's all you have, I'd like to get some sleep."

"It's not just a match," Zula replies. "It's a match that will never burn down and never go out."

"How?" Andra asks. "How is that possible?"

Zula looks at her with smug triumph. "I coated the match heads in a compound made from the lining of a salamander's lung—the same substance that's responsible for my own magic. It can't be consumed by fire, which means that these matches can stay lit forever and be relit as many times as you like."

"So what?" Kody asks.

"Just think—this could be the last match you ever need. The last one you ever *buy,*" Zula says. "How many people burn their wages in the form of matches and candles? How many of them would welcome the chance to put their money towards other purposes?"

Kody shakes his head and turns away. "I'm going to sleep."

"This is just the start!" Zula hastens to add. "I've got ideas, plans, models—don't pretend that this wouldn't make us rich."

He wheels on her. "Rich? Rich? You think that's what I want? When I was a soldier I could have had more wealth than I knew what to do with. Hell, we took just about this entire continent—do you really think I couldn't have kept my own share?" He points his hat at the match, which burns white in her hand like some minor solar emissary sent to keep watch over the mortal world. "That thing you're holding is a vulgarity," he says, "and I won't be a part of it. You think that's your fortune? Maybe you're right. But if you truly believe that, you'll pursue it without my help."

"I can't believe you," Zula says. "After all that you've done and for all that you are, you still want to play the romantic. Tell me what's vulgar about bringing magic to the people, Kody. We've been bringing them stories this whole time. Tell me why magic is different."

"Because," he bellows before calming himself and finishing in a sharp hiss, "a story is still a story after you tell it. When you take magic apart like that and put it back together again in a different shape, it's not magic anymore. Not in any way that's real."

"Since when do you care about what's real?" Zula counters.

But Kody doesn't respond. Instead he takes a blanket from one of the nearby Show wagons and, with that as his sole bedding, heads off into the night.

Zula stares after him for a moment or two. Then she holds the match upright inside the box and closes the lid so that the match is held in place. She sets the box down on the tailgate of the wagon and then climbs inside to sleep. Andra almost takes the whole thing then and there, box and match both, but she knows that Zula will look for it in the morning. Moreover, she knows that the box will be hers. She has seen it, and so it must be. Andra decides to bide her time and beds herself down with only her thoughts for company.

Though she will not say it, Andra disagrees with Kody and Zula. At present the Show is even less than a blurred reflection of its former self. Still Kody directs it to caper across the land like some battered marionette, laying itself down every night and rising again every morning.

Now that everyone else is gone, Andra's hands are the ones that pull the lines that make the Show move. Every day she feels the Show's weights and balances: in feeding the ones who need to be fed, in laying down stakes and pulling them up again, in disposing of that which needs to be disposed of, and in renewing all that calls for renewal. She knows now that the source of the Show's withering is not the Show itself, neither its nomadism nor its manufactured delirium nor its ever-shimmering phantasmagoria of exaggeration and fakery. The old Show could have survived if only its master had cared for it better. Absent such care, no new configuration of the Show would thrive.

Soon enough Andra's thoughts turn to her own concerns and she sleeps. When she wakens, the match is still alight: a final and futile symbol of Zula's rebuke.

II: The Threat of Her Undoing

The next day, they pass through the southern city proper. None of them has ever seen the like. Even in the capital the buildings were not so luxurious nor the people so lustrous. For some moments, Andra forgets Pol and what she has foreseen and is lost in the splendor of the city before her.

They pass villas decked with scrolled wood and surrounded by topiaries cut into the shapes of great birds and towering mammoths. They see a half-acre-wide building with unbroken stonework friezes for walls. Every intersecting street has some fountain or statuary at its center, and the roads are traveled by horse-drawn carriages that are larger than some of the homes they've seen in their travels.

Both on the road and among the working classes, the Show's beaten, sun-faded wagons had a charm and rakishness about them. Alongside these manors and mansions, they appear motley, makeshift, and short. Partway down a wide boulevard Kody stops at a building site. There he bargains with the foreman and trades the Show's remaining wagons for an unadorned but newer one, to which the foreman's workers transfer those articles that Kody deems necessary. He comes out of the deal with a small heap of coins as well, which he distributes evenly among the three of them. "It's all or nothing now—at least, for me. But if either of you want to call it quits," he says with a blunt look at Zula, "that should get you where you want to go."

Zula sneers at him. "You won't buy me off that easily," she says. "If I'm to be passed over for some sybaritic artiste, the least you owe me is the chance to see him for myself."

Near noon, they lunch on bread and salted fish beside a small park that overflows with lantana, athelas, coneflower, moly, and tickseed. Amid the greenery Zula challenges Kody again. "This has been a lovely sightseeing tour," she says, "but where's your poet? Do you plan to approach every door in the city until one of them reveals him or until we're expelled on charges of vagrancy?"

Andra answers before Kody has the chance to speak. "We'll find him on the beach," she says. She knows her time is coming. Her heart throbs in her chest and the food has no taste in her mouth. She shifts on the park wall and feels the tip of something pink her thigh. It is the seashell she was given, her memento of the old woman from her youth. Now it recalls Glyn to her as well, seated by the campfire and speaking of divine voices caged beneath the surface of the sea. She takes it in the palm of her hand. It comforts her. "One way or another, he'll meet us there."

"On the beach," Kody repeats as though he's known all along. "Just where I've been taking us."

"Did you plan to meet him at any particular place 'on the beach,' dear?" Zula asks of Andra. "At any particular time? Or were we just supposed to walk the miles back and forth in the hopes that we'll find him by pure happenstance?" She holds up a hand. "No, don't answer. It's a good thing you've left yourself some spare money, Kody, because you'll need all you can get once this foolish plan falls apart."

As they leave, Andra takes a fernflower on a whim and places it behind her ear. "Those are said to be guarded by evil spirits," Zula tells her disdainfully.

"Evil finds us all sooner or later in this world," Andra replies, placing the seashell back in her pocket. "To know its arrival in advance is a blessing, not a burden."

That silences Zula until they reach the coast half an

hour later. Unlike the even shoreline in the far north, the southern seaboard squirms and twists, now facing southeast, now due south, now nearly due west. The curl of sand before Kody, Andra, and Zula is clean and sunwashed and empty.

"Well done, Kody," Zula says. "You've dragged us straight across the Empire for a man who's not here. You have 'til sundown to decide: keep chasing phantoms or partner with me." As if to help him in his decision she presses her matchbox into his chest. "For now," she continues, "I leave the two of you to determine who is more the fool, the fool or the fool who follows her."

She turns her back on them and walks east, following the writhing coast. Kody watches her and sighs. "I really was hoping she'd snap out of it and stay. There would've been no point in having the freaks in a high-class Show, but fire can be sultry, enticing. She would've been a perfect fit with you and Pol. Hell—forget it. Let's just set up the tent. Maybe something'll come to me before she gets back."

***

Zula knows her opportunity is running thin. She, too, means to think of some winning remonstration by the time she and Kody are reunited. As she walks, the surf quells the planning of her future protestations. At length she finds herself at a remove from her own urgency, and from that remove she sees for the first time what she has positioned herself against.

Her time wandering the capital, back when the Show was whole, confirmed to her what she had been taught as a child: Work sustained the Empire, but progress—victory over geography, poverty, the cruder races, even nature itself—exalted and justified it. Kody may have drawn the

Empire's emblems on his wagons and flattered it in his tales, but Zula saw his Show as being no more substantial than the makeup that was washed away after every performance. Only the brilliance and daring of the Empire made the world rational; only the steady march of civilization and prosperity could call forth the future. The glaring poverty in the capital, the savagery of war, the hardships and hazards of taming the frontier—all these she understood to be the ingredients of history. Sharp and bitter though they may be, only by commingling them could her people acquire once and for all the elixir that would ease the woes of the world. Zula believed she would do her part and that she would be justly rewarded.

The southern city has troubled her certainties. It is no Imperial holding, no budding colony or province. Its wealth is a power that has been loosed from all fealty and reciprocity. *If this has been the game all along,* Zula realizes, *then everything else is a shadowplay.* Kody's ragtag Show, Zula's more orderly aspirations, the rise and fall of every village at a crossroad or creekside—all of it, she sees, is just the raucous slapstick that mollifies the rabble while the real show unfolds in secret behind gilded curtains.

It is in the grip of these thoughts, an hour or more along the beach, that she sees Pol. He is walking towards her, one bodyguard to each side save that facing the water. She knows who he is instantly. He wears only a pair of cloud-white linen pants with gold thread twined through the cuffs and seams. His body is bronzed and lithe, and he shows no signs of age. Zula remembers the beauty of the capital as beauty tamed and bent to the purpose of rule. When she saw it, she thought she would never see any beauty that surpassed it. She thought the same of the estates past which she just traveled and which were built for a raw and pure beauty. Pol, however, is another category outright. He is transcendent. For a moment, Zula suspects him of being an angel.

As he nears, she hears him testing couplet rhymes to the rhythm of the tide, as though he himself is the source and commander of its movement. To interrupt him requires a gathering of Zula's courage. "Are you the poet Pol?" she calls when he is only twenty or thirty feet away. The sound of her voice breaks his spell. He is not an angel. He is the threat of her undoing. She finds herself stalking towards him. "You are, aren't you? I'd have a word with you."

His guards bristle and move to intercept her, but Pol is relaxed. "Words are worth rather more to a poet than they are to the rest of the world. Why should I trade that which is worth a great deal to me for something that is self-evidently worth so little to you?"

"You stay away from Mister Pol, now, Miss," one of the guards warns her.

"Or what?" Zula spits. "Or he'll say something nasty about me using an intricate meter? I want to speak with him, I said, and by the burning god above I will."

The first of the stern-faced guards reaches her and clamps an arresting hand around her arm. "That's enough, Miss," he begins to say, but agony sears his hand and he jumps back.

"You oughtn't have done that," he says with a quiet satisfaction. He crouches, and within an eyeblink a thin dagger appears in his hand.

Yet Zula is faster still. She curls her fingers, and the man is clothed in white flame. His shrieks stun the other two guards into a moment's hesitation. Then they are upon him, their own blades dropped to the sand. Together the three of them stumble and flail into the ocean. They douse the flaming man as quickly as they are able, but it is too late. His skin has been melted into something that is not skin and his shock-numbed limbs shake uncontrollably. He moans and gibbers, and the sounds map an entire private vocabulary of pain.

Pol listens with an avid and professional curiosity. When the burned man finally quietens, he says, "Take him home, please."

"But Mister Pol —"

"Home," he repeats. "This charming woman and I will simply be having a little chat. You have nothing to fear."

The two unmutilated guards hesitate but do as he says. One of them looks hatefully at Zula as they pass, and then they are gone.

Pol stoops to retrieve their daggers from the sand. "I seem to have poor luck with the fairer sex," he says. "So few will simply give what is wanted, and so many demand that which will not be given. What is it that you want, Miss...?"

"I want to know whether you're the airy nothing I took you for when I first heard your name."

"And your conclusion, now that you've seen me?"

Zula sets her feet in the sand. "My conclusion is that you're even worse than I thought," she says. "What have you done to earn your place here? To merit the deference that your name inspires even in those who've never even laid eyes on you? What have you contributed?"

"Contributed?" Pol laughs. "Do you think the world is the fulcrum of some cosmic scale whose balance must forever be maintained? That each benefit one accrues must be counterposed by an equal act of self-sacrifice or meekness? My dear, remember the lessons of the ancient doctrines. Sol created animals *for us,* that the brave and the strong might take what we desire and thus approach godhood. Nothing exists but to be used as *we* see fit—that is, those of us who are willing to claim our proper birthright. There is no equilibrium, no golden proportion to imprison us. There is only a ladder, and our willingness to climb—or, should I say, only a larder, and our willingness to eat." He shrugs with the weapons still dangling from one hand. "Though, of course, there are always those who would rather be eaten."

A feather of fear drifts through Zula's chest. "So you admit it," she says. "You've created no tangible value, contributed nothing to the wealth of the world, brought us no closer to freedom."

"Value?" Pol asks himself. To Zula's surprise, he considers the question seriously. "I make no claims regarding value. The wealthy pay fortunes for my words. Commoners worship at my feet. That is all I need to know. Did the Emperor ponder the value of his Empire when he sent his armies to slaughter the barbarians of the plains? If so, it was certainly not the barbarians' values he bore in mind. Does the magnate tabulate value when deciding on his laborers' hours and pay? Or does he simply arrogate to himself the lion's share and leave the scraps for the others? You yourself—what did you 'contribute' to the beast from which you gained your pyromancy? Did you effect some trade or bargain with it, perhaps? Some equivalent exchange of 'value'? Naturally, you did no such thing. Nor should you have. The idea is absurd in itself. Why then should I be different?

"Consider that, when Sol took hold of the world so as to do his work, he did so over and against the protestations of the lesser gods. Consider that he eventually shattered their very voices and sank their divine protestations below the sea. Can we mortals claim to judge the value of such an act? No—it is only for us to follow the one example or the other. Power or powerlessness. Might or misery. The virtue of reciprocity is a seductive heresy. Its only proponents are weaklings and those made light-headed by sentiment."

Zula says nothing. Again she senses something other-worldly in Pol, some fearful glamor, as of an actor descended from a great stage to mingle among the ignorant multitude. The sand under their feet, once damp, has now dried, as though the very waves have shied away from his surety.

"I see I've exhausted your store of words," he says. "As predicted, mine were the sturdier. I leave you now to whatever business you choose to pursue. May the light of the great god Sol shine always upon you."

He walks past her, and still Zula says nothing. Only when she fears that he will disappear behind a curve in the coastline does she turn and call to him. "Then what's to stop me?"

Pol looks back over his shoulder. "Stop you?"

"What's to stop me from taking whatever I want by whatever means I can?" Her face is set in anger. There are tears in her eyes. "What's to stop me from following you back to your home and burning it to the ground just to show the world what your arrogance truly buys?"

Now Pol turns to face her fully. His expression is that of a tutor delighted by his student's sudden progress. "What's to stop you?" he asks. Then he vanishes.

Zula stares at the blank sand where Pol stood. She inhales, and at the tip of her breath she feels the edge of a blade at her throat.

"I am," his voice says in her ear.

She feels him now, his body lightly pressed against the back of her shirt, his breath soft on her shoulder. She did not mean for it to come this far. She did not mean anything. Her words carried no more purpose or plan than her tears. She is not ready to die.

She calls the fire to her, but Pol is too quick. At the first lick of heat he jabs one long fingernail into the place where Zula's neck meets her skull. Something burns and tingles there, the sting of a wasp, and her tears abruptly stop. Her breathing slows. Her body softens.

"You should be proud of yourself," Pol tells her. "For a moment you grasped the truth, even if in the end you were too weak to hold it."

Thoughts fall from Zula's mind like leaves from a parched and dying tree. She forgets why she has come here. She forgets those she has left behind. She forgets her own name.

"I understand," Pol says. "Fear is the great weakness of our kind: fear of failure, fear of jealousy, fear of censure. You needn't fear those things any longer. You needn't fear anything at all."

She nods. From someplace close there comes a comforting hush. Her head tilts towards the sea.

"Yes, yes!" Pol says happily. "Now do you see how lovely the world can be without fear? The water is so very beautiful. You'd like to go there, wouldn't you?"

She nods.

"Then go!" he says, and releases her.

As she shuffles forward, Pol checks the dagger for blood. Seeing none on the blade, he licks his fingernail clean. He checks the position of the sun in the sky and weighs the weapons in his hand. Judging it to be too early to return home for the evening, he decides to continue his walk.

Still holding the daggers, he rounds a bend to the west and moves out of sight. Behind him the water covers the

pyromancer's chest. Unafraid, she walks deeper into the
sea.

★★★

By the time Pol reaches the tent, the sun is nearly touching
the horizon. Coming from the east, he sees the back of the
tent first. Its presence intrigues him as quickly and completely as it would a child. It is enchanting in its incon-
gruity; its hidden face draws him near. Kody could not
have planned it better himself, though he is not the one
who chose the site. Andra did that, just as in the inter-
vening hours it was Andra who arranged the rug and the
cot and the chairs, and Andra who laid the four artifacts of
her vision on a chest facing the sea: the piton, the tooth,
the scale, the matchbox.

"Good thinking," Kody said when he saw them. "I
always find that a few good knickknacks lend an air of
discernment to a room. They get the mind going, keep
folks distracted and suggestible. In fact, I think I'll cheat
back to the wagon and grab a few of my own. Hold the
fort, will you?"

That was no more than a minute ago. Now Andra
hears the sand-softened footfalls of Pol's approach. She
hopes that Kody was right and that her fraudulent arsenal
will induce Pol to drop his guard. Her skin tingles and her
pulse thumps in her throat, the fanfare and pedal drum to
announce what must for her sake be the greatest trick of
her life. She has had no opportunities to rehearse. There
will be no second engagement. Whichever advantages present themselves to her, she must take them now.

The footsteps travel the side of the tent and cross to
where the flaps have been pinned back, one on each side.
He pauses, silhouetted against the gold-lit sea and the

gaudy opulence of the setting sun.

"Hello, Pol," Andra says. "All of this is for you, so the least you could do is come in."

He chuckles. "This is a most interesting evening indeed. You're the second strange woman I've met today who knows my name. The first tried to burn me alive." Andra thinks of Zula and her heart leaps in her chest, but she does not dare break character or depart from the script. "Now the second invites me into her tent," Pol continues, "which she says she's pitched for me alone. There is a delicious symbolism at work here, or I am not half the poet I take myself to be."

Saying this, he enters the tent, and Andra sees him properly. "I admit that I am strange," she says, "but no stranger than a man who wears the face and body of a man much younger than he is."

Pol pauses with his hand on the chair opposite Andra. He thinks for a moment, then sits. The laughter has gone out of him. In each of his hands, a dagger waits. "So you know more than my name."

"I know many things," Andra replies.

"Then you must know that there's nothing you can take from me by either force or guile."

Andra smiles at him as though he is a boastful child. "There's nothing you have that I could ever want." The words are true. The soft pity in them is not. She fears him with an intensity that borders on hunger, a nerve-wracked appetite that sharpens as she feeds it.

"Then why?" Pol asks. "Why all this?"

She waits. Behind Pol the sun descends below sand and sea. "Because," she says, "of what you took from me."

He observes everything closely now: the tent and its furnishings, the artifacts arrayed on the chest, the woman seated across from him. "I know you," he says at last.

"We've met before. You're the soothsayer, aren't you? From the desert town?"

Andra nods.

"This is an unexpected reunion indeed," Pol says, and his face contorts with cruel pleasure. "I haven't thought of you in nearly thirty years. But I see you've thought of me. The pyromancer—was she your agent?"

"No. I have no use for an agent. What comes next has been preordained. Only I can undo what has been done."

A maniac delight shines in Pol's eyes. "And how do you plan to do that? Beg?" He gestures to the four artifacts on the chest. "Barter with me using these cheap trinkets? Or, no—I have it. You would challenge me to a duel of magic, and these items represent your armory of powers." With one dagger he points to the tooth, then the matchbox. "Lightning at sunset! Fire at dawn!"

He laughs, but then he sees Andra's expression. "It *is* a duel, isn't it?" he says. "I admire your bravery and your persistence, old woman, but there are far easier deaths than the one you've chosen."

"It was never a choice," Andra replies. "I understand that now. Choice is a luxury reserved for the strong. You make sure of that, you and those like you. Still, there is balance. Where the land ends, the water begins. No matter how long the season of growth is, the season of death always waits close by. And even those who lift their hands to praise the sun's infinite light must still take their rest in the dark."

Pol opens his mouth to issue some snarling rejoinder, but Andra cuts him off before he can speak. "Yes, Pol, even now the hidden stagehands of the world are rearranging the scene to bring it about. Balance between day and night, between power and frailty, between wealth and need. Between you and me. But you mistake me. These are not my weapons," she says, and she holds out her hand. The tiny seashell rests there, in her upturned palm. "This is."

Quickly, before Pol can make sense of what he's seen, Andra opens her mouth and places the seashell on her tongue. She feels the nubs on its tip and the soft sweep of its median. It tastes of brine and age, and it is too large for her to swallow. Her preamble is over. There is nothing left to do but make the leap.

"Pol, you who would raise yourself to the sky and live as a god," she says, her voice rounded and deepened from speaking around the shell, "now is the moment you become a child of the soil again."

As she speaks, she feels she is being drawn backward and down as though standing in the outward flow of the ebb tide. Panic rises in her like stage fright, but she neither rushes nor resists. She only allows herself to fall.

What she falls into is herself. There she finds a well of power deep enough to drown a mountain, broad enough to subsume a continent, and unquenchable. She sees its immeasurable vastness, and feels its currents and tributaries as clearly as she does the blood in her palms and the breath in her lungs.

The ebbing slackens, slows, stops. Nothing has been lost, she feels. Nothing has been diminished. It has only been gathered. Inside her, the magic holds itself in total stillness. And then it begins to swell.

As it climbs itself crest by crest, Andra realizes that she no longer feels the shell on her tongue. In its place she tastes saltwater. She swallows it down and speaks again, and the magic floods her and floods the tent and sweeps Pol aloft as though he were no more than a grain of sand.

"I never wanted this," Andra says, and ten thousand whispered voices speak with her. "The powers you have, the wealth you seek, all the glories and adorations that the world piles before you—I never wanted any of it."

She stands, and the magic bears her forward like a wave. "I only wanted a home. But you took that from me, because you don't know what a home is."

Her words crash over him now, heavy as the sea. He gasps for air. "Please," he says, choking out each word, "don't hurt me."

Andra sobs, and a hundred thousand hushed wails accompany her. "To hurt is yours," an ancient anguished chorus cries through Andra's mouth. "To divide is yours. To take is yours. Every one of your powers is stolen, every one of your accomplishments won only for your benefit and enjoyed by you alone. Yours is indeed the Light of the Sun: a jealous light that wipes all others from the sky; a harsh and implacable light that draws the eye only to blind it. Yes, Pol, and a pitiable light as well, because you stand alone not in your strength but in order to deny those things that all know to be inescapable. There was darkness at the beginning of the world, tiny mage, and every heart knows that there will be darkness at its end. Even yours.

"But I am not here to be your end," Andra says, and for a moment her voice is hers alone and the magic in the air reaches a fluid, shifting equipoise. "I'm not here for you at all. I'm here for myself, so that I can finally reclaim the life that is mine." Her powers ebb again, gently now. Before they go she speaks one last time, and countless sorrowed voices join hers. "Let us return to the way we were made," they say. "Soft and vulnerable, awestruck and needful, with no magics to save or condemn us. Let it all wash away, and let us be clean."

Then, there is only the sound of the ocean. Andra feels wetness at her feet. She looks down and sees sea-water, though the shoreline is a hundred feet away or more. When she looks up again, she sees Pol. But it is not the Pol she knows. He is gray-haired and sallow and decrepit, and there is no sign of power on his skin or in the way he holds himself.

Inside Andra there is likewise nothing, neither curse nor boon. Her clairvoyance, never truly hers but only ever Pol's constant hex, has been dissolved along with his other magics; and in effecting that dissolution, the seashell's enchantment was swept up as well, becoming its own cancellation.

The two of them breathe for a moment, Pol trembling in his chair, Andra looking down on him. A low sound of desolation starts in his throat. He reaches for his daggers but they are gone, swept out to sea. He swings his head upward and screams and grabs the piton from atop the chest.

Andra does not think to fight. Everything she has done, she has done so that she would not have to fight. Pol lunges around the chest to her right. She makes for the left side of the chest, but her feet tangle in the sand and she closes her eyes as she falls.

A moment later there is the sound of flesh meeting flesh. Two bodies hit the ground, and two men grunt. Andra opens her eyes to see Kody sitting astride Pol, holding his neck with one hand and twisting the piton free with the other. Pol is still shrieking, but Kody talks over him, saying, "Hey! Hey, now! Quit it! I don't know who in the hell you are or what you think you're doing here, but I've killed stronger than you and lived to tell about it. Quit squirming, you little rat! Quit!"

At the last word, Pol twists one way, Kody twists him the other, and there is a popping noise. Pol's screams suddenly go quiet. Kody stands and slides the piton into a pocket and spits on the ground. "Damn! I warned him. I told him to quit."

He looks down as though he means to kick the dead body. Instead he turns to Andra and says, "Who in the name of god was that, anyway? What was he even doing here?"

Andra places one hand on the chest and stands. "That was Pol," she says, "the Light of the Sun, the Empire's greatest poet and proudest mage."

"That's not funny," Kody says.

"No," Andra agrees, "it's not," and then she starts to cry.

Kody looks at her, then at the corpse on the ground. "No," he says. "No, no, no, no. What happened to him, Andra? What did you do? He was young and beautiful— they all said so, they all told me. Andra, what did you do? You ruined me. You ruined my Show. You ruined every- thing!"

"Kody, I'm sorry—please believe me. I wish I'd had a choice, but it had to be this way."

He looks up. "Did you plan this—all of this? Jorg and Glyn and all the rest—did you do all that just to get me here?"

She shakes her head, horrified at the thought. "No, Kody, I would never—"

"All those visions," he says, "they never were real, were they? I knew I shouldn't've listened to you! From day one I knew you didn't care about the Show. You were always trying to cover for people, make excuses for them, tell me all kinds of stories. Nobody else believed you, but I thought I knew better!" He stares out of the tent opening. Behind the water, twilight is gently disassembling the great exposition of the day. Kody slams his fist against her chair and it topples softly to the ground. "Why him? Why do all this just to ruin one man?"

Andra wants to tell him about her vision. She wants to

say it was all fated for her. But she knows he no longer believes. "We had a past," she says instead.

"And that was worth all this?" Kody asks, disgusted. "Worth his life, worth Jorg's life, worth lying to me and the world for all these years?"

"I am sorry, Kody, truly," Andra says sadly, "but you were right: The best part of being in a show is that anyone who accuses you of lying is just accusing you of doing your job."

Her words take the fight out of Kody. "Get out," he tells her. "Get out and leave me to what's left of my life and pray to whatever gods you hold sacred that I never see you again."

Andra hesitates for just an instant. She knows where she intends to go, and she wants to invite him to come with her. But the time for such reconciliation is over, if ever there had been one. Quietly she slips past him, and then she is through the tent door and into the night.

A Homecoming

The season has changed by the time Andra reaches the northern coast again. Her return was the first journey in her life that she undertook without her curse; her only visions were those trembling desires spun from her hope. She has bought her way north one caravan at a time, and in doing so she has spent nearly all of Kody's final payment to her. Along the way she has performed for no one, though she has given free counsel to the few who both needed and accepted it. Now, she walks the last half-mile to the coast, smelling salt-water and young blossoms in the calefying spring morning.

She hears the tiny community before she sees it. There is woodwork and conversation and the beat of outsized wings, and her hope begins to bloom into belief.

She sees Glyn and several goblins first. Together they bend down to cultivate a plot of raised garden beds that are located just above the sandline. From ten or twenty yards off she hails them. The goblins are dove-gray in the morning light and sheened with sweat. They run to her and she kneels to greet them.

"We knew you'd be back," Tom tells her.

The others nod. "We saw you standing in the water back then and we knew," Cate adds.

"How did you know?" Andra asks. The answer makes no difference to her. She simply wants to hear their voices.

"Those who are free to seek their home will always find it," Jack answers, and Andra's only response is to enfold her in her arms.

As they walk together towards the beds, Andra crests the shoreline and sees their warren. The goblins have built it around one of the upshore pilings of the pier. On its domed roof, young grass germinates. Behind, on the pier itself, Nickelette's house has grown and is growing still.

Andra thinks that she can make out Jorg supervising Etain and another small group of goblins.

Glyn calls out to her as she and her group of goblins pass the garden beds. "Is Kody with you?" he asks.

"No," she calls back. "I don't think he'll be coming here again."

Only then does Glyn join her, and together they reunite with Jorg and Etain and the rest of the goblins where the pier meets the land. When they ask for her story, she tells them only that she, Zula, and Kody fell out and parted ways. They talk for a few minutes more, then Jorg sends the others back to work.

"Come," he says as the pier empties, "let me introduce you to Nic."

Andra observes him as they walk down to the beach. He looks older than he did in the Show but healthier as well. Some strength has returned to his arms and his back, and he moves with an acceptance of his place in the world: above the soil, below the sky. "I'm sorry for poisoning you," Andra says to him.

He waves her away. "You saved my life."

"I hope you think it was worth saving."

Jorg stops on the sand and looks down at his half-devoured hand. "If it wasn't then," he says, "it is now." He raises his head. "Come on. Nic's been waiting to meet you."

They find Nickelette making a close survey of Cary's right inner wing. When she hears their footsteps in the sand she turns and grins and puts her hands on her hips. "I wish you'd trained this big old lug better," she says to Jorg. "All I'm trying to do is give him an examination and he keeps moving all around."

Jorg smiles back. "Maybe he's just ticklish. But let that aside for now. I want to introduce you to someone, Nic. This is Andra, our fortuneteller. Or, well—not 'our' anymore."

"And not a fortuneteller, either," Andra says, and she holds out her hand.

Nickelette shakes it. "I've heard a lot about you," she says. "You just about turned me into a hotelier, from the way Jorg, Etain, and Glyn tell it. I'd been hoping I might get to hear your version."

"I'll leave you two to catch up," Jorg says. "It's about time that we stock up on fish anyway. Let's go, Cary." He whistles and walks back along the beach towards the pier. Cary shakes his head, rises into the air, and follows his friend.

"It's a long story," Andra says once the sand has settled.

"I'll bet. Maybe you'll tell it someday."

Andra nods. "Maybe. In the meantime, would you object to adding an old, useless woman to your guests?"

"Aw, hell," Nickelette says, "I haven't met anybody useless yet, and I sure doubt that you're the first. Between my research, all the new mouths to feed, and trying to make peace with the locals, there's always something to do." She smiles again. "I'm sure you'll fit right in somewhere or other."

"Thank you," Andra says, and she looks away. "I'll try my best to make it worth your while, but, given my experiences with my last employer, I can't make any promises."

Nickelette laughs out loud. "Oh, please—'employer'

this, 'worth your while' that. That's the way they do things out there." She gestures broadly south, in the direction of the capital and the Empire at large. "If I wanted to be that way I would've never come out here to begin with. I don't 'employ' nobody. We're trying something new here—or maybe something old, but something different, anyway. Whatever future's out there for us, nobody knows what it is. I hope that's alright with you."

"Quite honestly," Andra says, "I think it sounds perfect."

And together, Nickelette reaching to steady Andra's steps, the two women walk back to the pier, and home.

ACKNOWLEDGMENTS

I have no way of properly recognizing everyone who has contributed to this book. There may be some writers whose paths are smooth; if so, I'm not one of them, and I've needed a good deal of help along the way.

I should first thank my family. Evelyn Horowitz, my grandmother, is a natural storyteller, and Howard Lupovitz, my grandfather, had dreams of publishing his own writing. I'm proud to carry on their legacy. I also want to thank my parents, Michael and Laura, for allowing me to have a bookish childhood and nurturing both my imagination and my sense of purpose.

Thanks are also due to Adam Reger and Beth Townsend for helping me to understand the distance between my ego and my abilities, and for helping me to narrow that gap. Thank you also to the members of the Fighting Game Community who read and supported my early work, especially Henry Choi, who first made me a paid writer. And thank you to Dan Lupovitz, my uncle, for understanding the creative process and offering the type of encouragement that I didn't know how to find anywhere else.

With *Kody* in particular, I should thank my early readers as well as my editor for their feedback and insights. These people include my ludicrously brilliant sister Ariel; my wonderfully kind aunt, Terry Smith; and my dear friends Chris Borges and Pat Schober. Their support and honesty are a constant source of assurance. And, of course, Michael Takeda's efforts on behalf of Pink Narcissus Press have been vital. I hope sincerely that my work reflects well on them, and I'm obliged to inform you, the reader, that any remaining shortcomings in this text are mine and not theirs.

Most of all, I have to thank my wife, Julie, without whom I would be unrecognizable to myself. It would take another fifty thousand words to say how grateful I am that I can rely on her and be the one on whom she can rely; comfort her and be the one she comforts; and grow together with her. Though the words are mine, this book is in a real way her accomplishment as well, because she was my heart when I was too hurt or scared to trust my own.